THE DRAGON PRINCE

D1569897

THE DRAGON & PRINCE

STORIES AND LEGENDS
FROM VIETNAM

Thich Nhat Hanh

**PARALLAX
PRESS**

BERKELEY, CALIFORNIA

Parallax Press
P.O. Box 7355
Berkeley, California 94707
parallax.org

Parallax Press is the publishing division
of Plum Village Community of
Engaged Buddhism, Inc.

Illustrations by Nguyen Thi Hop
and Nguyen Dong.
Cover design by Graciela Galup.
Text design by Gopa & Ted2, Inc.

All stories in this book were translated
from the Vietnamese by Mobi Warren
except: "The Pine Gate," Vo Dinh Mai
and "A Bouquet of Wildflowers," Dinh
Nghiem.

Books in which the stories originally
appeared: "The Pine Gate" and "The
Ancient Tree" in *The Pine Gate* (Fredo-
nia, NY: White Pine Press, 1987); "A
Bouquet of Wildflowers" in *The Stone
Boy* (Berkeley, CA: Parallax Press,
1996); all others in *A Taste of Earth* (Berkeley, CA: Parallax Press, 1993). The
Afterword from *Van Lang di su*, 1974,
appears here in English for the first
time.

Library of Congress Cataloging-in-Publication Data

Nhât Hanh, Thích.
  [Van Lang di su. English]
  The Dragon Prince : stories and legends from Vietnam / Thich Nhat Hanh.
    p. cm.
  Previously published: A taste of earth, and other legends of Vietnam, ©1993; also
includes stories previously published elsewhere.
  ISBN 978-1-888375-74-9
  1. Legends—Vietnam. 2. Tales—Vietnam. I. Title.
  GR313.N4813 2007
  398.209597—dc22
                                                              2007012018

MR

CONTENTS

Conflict and Change

ᶜᵀRANSLATOR'S NOTE

THIS RETELLING of traditional Vietnamese legends by Thich Nhat Hanh was first published in Vietnam in the fall of 1974 under the title *The Extraordinary Legends of Van Lang (Van Lang di su)*. At that time, I was working as a volunteer with the Vietnamese Buddhist Peace Delegation in Paris, headed by Thich Nhat Hanh, and so I had the privilege of being present as he was writing these stories. I remember the many hours of scrupulous research he devoted to ancient Vietnamese anthropology and history. He wanted the stories to accurately describe the early centuries of Vietnam's development. He did most of the actual writing in his hermitage 100 miles to the south, returning to Paris with a thick notebook filled with line after line of careful and extremely neat handwriting.

Thich Nhat Hanh showed a great interest in Western children's literature (*Winnie the Pooh* and *The Wind in the Willows* were among his favorites) and was impressed by the wide array of books devoted to children in the West. He regretted that there were not more Vietnamese books written especially for children. He also expressed a concern that many Western children's books overemphasized the dichotomy between good and bad. With war raging in Vietnam, he felt a responsibility to offer children stories that reflected themes of understanding and reconciliation, stories that pointed away from the futility of dualistic "war-thinking" and in the direction of thinking based on cooperation and healing. Thich Nhat Hanh was also interested in showing the influence of India on early Vietnamese culture, often overlooked because of the more obvious influence of China. To introduce the themes of both reconciliation and India, he created the character of Princess Sita, a daughter of the Dragon Prince. She appears in two of these stories: "The Voyage" and "Princess Sita."

In the afterword in the original Vietnamese edition, two young flood relief workers discuss the addition of a new character to otherwise traditional stories. One of them says, "The personality of Sita has just been created. Who knows if she will be admitted into the pantheon of Vietnamese gods."

The other worker answers, "Why not? Mythology is created by people. The people who lived long ago are like the people who live today. Myth was created to explain the universe and humanity's place in it. Myths are not simply creations of the imagination with no relation to reality. At the archaeological site of Thanh Oc, thousands of copper arrows were recently excavated. That means that the legend of the magic bow in 'The Spiral Palace' must have had some relation to actual events during King An Duong's rule. Princess Sita is also a reality. In the present war, we have seen countless people working for reconciliation who face great danger and share the suffering of those who are wounded, just like Princess Sita. In the traditional telling of the battle between the gods Son Vuong and Thuy Vuong, the presence of someone like Sita has been forgotten. To remember her is to continue the work of creation. Without her, the story of Son Vuong and Thuy Vuong would not be complete."

Unlike many collections of folktales and legends that seem to emerge from a timeless place, this collection unfolds as a history.

While the stories can be read and enjoyed individually, it's even more satisfying to read them in order.

For instance, a shift from a culture based on matriarchal values to one based on patriarchal values takes place between the first section, "Beginnings," and the second section, "Customs and Culture." In the beginning, the goddess Au Co served as the people's leader. Married couples remained with the wife's family. Dragon Emperor, father to the people, was affectionately called Lac Dragon, after the celestial bird associated with the goddess. When Dragon Emperor returns to his duties beneath the sea and Au Co retires to the lofty mountains, a new order is introduced and a male king is chosen to rule. Thus begins the section on "Culture and Customs." The boy Hung, who travels beneath the sea in "The Voyage," becomes King Hung Vuong I, and his companion Mi becomes the first queen. Thereafter married couples live with the groom's family—a reference to this is in "The Areca Tree"—and children take their father's name. Some aspects of the goddess were retained, however. The Lac bird remained the country's symbol, and kingdom officials were bestowed with titles that included the term "Lac" to continually remind the people of their Goddess Mother.

Myth, anthropology, ancient history, the simple joys of peace, and the sorrows of war can all be found in *The Dragon Prince*. Throughout, the heroes and heroines of the stories celebrate closeness to the earth, the importance of assuming personal responsibility for one's conduct, and the possibilities of resolving conflict through understanding rather than violence—themes as compelling today as they were to the first tellers of these tales.

But let the stories speak for themselves. Savor the tastes, fragrances, sights, and sounds of an older, distant world, a world that can delight and inspire.

—Mobi Warren

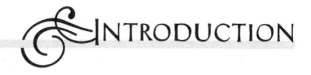

INTRODUCTION

VIETNAMESE CULTURE goes back some 4000 years, according to legend and archeological evidence. Bronze Age civilizations appeared in several river valleys of present-day North Vietnam at the end of the third millennium B.C.E. This culminated in the Dong Son culture of the seventh to the first century B.C.E. which scholars consider to be the time during which Vietnamese national traditions developed. This period is also associated with the first line of Vietnamese monarchs, the legendary Hung kings. The reign of the Hung kings has become interwoven with the mythic tradition of Vietnam.

According to the Vietnamese creation myth, the Dragon Prince, Lac Long Quan, and the heavenly spirit, Au Co, are the founders of Vietnam and the progenitors of the Vietnamese people. The dragon prince came out of the sea. Au Co came to earth as a bird and she is associated with the mountains. Their union can be seen as symbolic of the union of land and sea, the geographical areas essential to Vietnamese life and culture. The Dragon Prince and Au Co had one hundred children. Their eldest son became the first Hung king, King Hung Vuong, who was succeeded by seventeen more Hung monarchs, each of whom was said to have reigned for 150 years over the kingdom of Van Lang. Their influence, however, extended much farther, due to a relationship of mutual support with the Lac lords who ruled at the village, and sometimes regional, level. The influence of the Hung kings was said to have reached from Southern China to Central Vietnam.

Vietnamese recorded history begins in the third century B.C.E. when the last Hung king was defeated by Thuc Phan, who had come with a wave of migration of the Au Viet people from the north. He became another legendary king, An Duong Vuong, and the Lac Viet and Au Viet civilizations joined in the new kingdom of Au Lac. Although these invaders had come from Southern China, rule of Au Lac was autonomous from China. King An Duong Vuong was deposed by the Chinese general Trieu Da who became the first king of the Trieu dynasty, Trieu Vu Vuong. This dynasty lasted seventy years, until the Chinese invasion. The Trieu court adopted Vietnamese customs and their rule remained essentially independent of China, although China's influence was growing during this time.

In 111 B.C.E. Vietnam was invaded by China. Chinese dominance lasted over one thousand years. During this period there were many uprisings, some quite successful. But it wasn't until 939 C.E. that the Vietnamese people finally succeeded in driving the Chinese out of Vietnam.

The Vietnamese mythic tradition has been influenced by contact with many people and cultures. A significant influence has been that of China and of the struggle against Chinese domination. Another significant influence has been that of Indian legends and Buddhism.

Vietnamese people lived for the most part as farmers or fishermen in small villages or family settlements. Some of their pre-Buddhist beliefs were of Grandfather Sky who was up in the heavens and was able to see clearly everything that was happening on Earth. He was able to punish those who did wrong and help those who did good.

Grandfather Sky, although very powerful, was not seen as responsible for the whole of creation, so he should not be seen as the god of the monotheistic religions. Grandfather Sky had underlings near and far. Close by was Grandfather Thunder and Old Woman Lightning. Far away was the spirit of mountain, the spirit of water, the spirit of the banyan tree, the Kitchen god, Grandfather Earth, and the spirit of Mount Tan Vien.

Tombs from the first century B.C.E. have been excavated in Lach Truong, Thanh Hoa Province. Some of these tombs are painted with pictures of the Thay Mo—the medium who was able to be in touch with the world of the dead—dressed in bird feathers, symbolic of the ability to move between worlds, and also recalling the bird who along with the dragon, was seen as the founder of the Vietnamese people.

The legend of a dragon living in the sea probably grew from Vietnamese fishermen diving and being injured by sea creatures which they thought to be a dragon. The fishermen painted themselves to make the dragon afraid, and they came to see themselves as the race of the dragon.

This is the setting into which Indian merchants and monks brought Buddhism to Vietnam beginning in the first century C.E. The teachings of cause and effect and of karma were very much in accord with the idea of Grandfather Sky. The teaching of the cycle of rebirth was in accord with the existing idea of a soul that is able to continue after the corpse has disintegrated. This teaching was also in harmony with the luxurious growth of plant life observable in this hot and humid country.

The Vietnamese hadn't yet become loyal devotees of Confucianism or Taoism, and they were not held by solid systems of thought, so Buddhism penetrated Vietnamese civilization as naturally and easily as water penetrates the earth. The ancient treasury of Vietnamese literature gathered together elements of legends from former lives of the Buddha. The story of Tam Cam is a story about cause and effect and karma. In this story, Buddha plays the role of Grandfather Sky, who is able to see all the injustices that are happening on the earth.

A special characteristic of the Vietnamese language is that it does not contain the word "I" or "you." Before a Vietnamese person can talk to someone, we have to establish our relationship with them. We call them mother, father, aunt, uncle, grandparent, older or younger brother or sister, niece, or nephew. This means we see our-selves not as "I," but as niece, nephew, grandchild, older or younger brother or sister, daughter, son, uncle, or aunt. Nobody is a stranger; everyone we meet is addressed as a family member. Each person is a part of the larger community, and the community exists in us. If a younger sister falls, an older sister or brother will pick her up. There is a Vietnamese saying about this, "The healthy leaf covers and protects the torn leaf."

In these stories, you will find these unique characteristics of Viet-namese culture that our way of living has created. Are the stories Buddhist? Yes and no. Indian merchants sometimes asked a monk to accompany them on the long sea voyage to Vietnam. The monks and traders spent several months in Vietnam while they waited for the trade winds that would take them home. During this time they lived their devotional lives in Vietnam as monks or laypeople. For the traders this meant observing the Five Precepts: not killing, stealing, committing sexual misconduct, telling lies, or drinking alcohol. They had faith in the teaching of cause and effect, and therefore they took care to make offerings and practice generosity, especially making the offering of food, robes, and lodging to monks.

The Buddhist ideas of accumulating merit, simple living, *karuna* (compassion), *karma* (rebirth and retribution), and the importance of *sangha* (community) are all present in many of these stories, but perhaps you will be so absorbed in the lives and adventures told here that you will not notice them. That is just fine. These stories are not lectures. They are here to be savored, so please take your time with them and enjoy a little bit of Vietnam.

BEGINNINGS

THE DRAGON PRINCE

L ONG AGO, when earth and sky were still covered in
darkness, a great bird with wings like curtains of night
came to rest on the cold earth. She sat for millions of
years without stirring, until at last she laid two enormous eggs—one
red, the other ivory. Powerful gusts of wind from her majestic wings
shook heaven and earth as she flew back into the deep reaches of
space.

Thousands of years later, the red egg began to glow. Bright light
poured from the egg, chasing away the dense fog that had covered
the mountains and filled the valleys for so long. With a thunderous
clap, the red egg cracked, freeing a fiery golden crow whose brilliant
light dazzled sky and earth.

Then the ivory egg began to radiate a soft and gentle light, and it,
too, cracked open. Its shell burst into many fine pieces as an enormous, graceful swan emerged and flew into the sky, tender light
streaming from her body down onto the earth.

Each bird followed its own course as it circled the earth. Soft, cool
light streamed gently down from the wild swan. The golden crow's
fiery wings hurled sparks of bright fire into space as it cried like
thunder. The sparks remained suspended in the heavens, twinkling

like diamonds. For millions of years, cold darkness had reigned. Now these wondrous birds brought the comfort of light.

The crow's red hot shell exploded into flames that burned for seven years. Boulders melted into fine sand, creating a vast desert. Steam rose from the seas and formed a blanket of clouds that shielded the earth from the crow's fiercest rays. The heavens reeled in the rich aroma that rose from the newly warmed earth.

The light shone all the way to the 36th heaven, where lived many goddesses. The youngest and loveliest goddess, Au Co, pulled back a curtain of cloud, saw the rosy earth below encircled by a halo of light, and cried, "Come, my sisters, let us change ourselves into white Lac birds and fly down to explore this new planet!"

Without hesitation, the goddesses transformed themselves into snow-white birds and flew down to the rosy earth. It was truly a wonderful discovery. As Lac birds they flew over the emerald sea, surprised to see their own reflections dancing in the water. The warm light of the golden crow was delightful. They leisurely skimmed over the pink mountains and came to rest on a hillside covered with soil as fine as powder.

When the first bird touched the ground, she folded her wings and returned to her goddess form. The other goddesses followed her example. Never had the earth hosted so delightful an event! The goddesses laughed and sang as, hand in hand, they strolled up and down the pink slopes. The earth beneath their feet was as soft as cotton balls. When they reached a broad meadow, they began to dance. It was the first dancing on earth. Before that moment, dancing had only been known in the 36th heaven. After a time, Au Co broke away from her sisters, knelt down to examine the fragrant earth more closely, and scooped up a small handful. How soft it was! How good it smelled! The other goddesses paused from their dancing and they too scooped up handfuls of pink earth.

Suddenly Au Co wondered if the earth tasted as good as it smelled, and she lifted her hand to her mouth. Another goddess shouted, "Au Co! Don't do that!" But it was too late. Au Co had already swallowed a tiny handful of the sweet earth. The goddess who had shouted broke away from the others and ran towards Au Co. She grabbed the young goddess by the hand.

"Au Co, you foolish one! I'm afraid what you have done can never be repaired. Ours is the realm of form, not the realm of desire."

Frightened, the other goddesses quickly brushed all particles of pink earth from their delicate hands. They gathered around Au Co.

"What should we do now?" asked one.

"Let's leave at once and not mention our outing to anyone," suggested another.

They noticed with alarm that it was growing dark. The golden crow had almost disappeared behind the mountains and the light was fading with him.

"We must return before the golden crow disappears!" cried one goddess. She bent over slightly and transformed herself again into a snow-white Lac bird. The others did the same. As they flew into the sky their wings seemed to wave regretful farewells to the lovely earth.

Light disappeared with the golden crow, but it wasn't long before the wild swan returned. Her cool and gentle light was a refreshing change from the bright and sometimes burning rays of the golden crow. The first day on Earth had just ended. It lasted as long as seven of our years today. Now the first night was beginning. It was a pleasant and mild night, illuminated by the swan's tender light.

Beneath that light, Au Co flew frantically back and forth, unable to join her sisters. Her wings were too heavy, and no matter how hard she tried, she could fly no higher. Because Au Co had tasted the new earth, she had lost her magical flying powers and could no longer return to the 36th heaven. Frightened and alone, she sank back down to earth. She resumed her goddess form and leaned against a boulder to weep.

Throughout the night, her tears became a long river that wound down to the seashore, where it emptied into the sea. Beneath the waves, multitudes of small creatures—shrimp, crabs, fish, and oysters—tasted the new current of water perfumed with fragrant earth. They shared their discovery with Dragon Prince, the son of the Sea Dragon Emperor, who had turned himself into a small fish to follow the sweet current upstream in search of its source. Although he swam swiftly, the first night on earth ended before he reached shore.

When Dragon Prince lifted his head above the water, he could see the golden crow. The sparkling sea rivaled his father's emerald palace below. Lapping waves spewed foam as white as snow. The prince leaped into the air. How soft, clear, and immense the sky was—round and blue like the sea itself. He could see the pale outlines of mountains and hills shimmering in the distance. Everything was similar to the landscape beneath the sea, yet here the world seemed more expansive, lighter and clearer.

He jumped onto shore and turned himself into a handsome young man with a broad forehead, long legs, and eyes that shone like stars. As he strolled along the shore, he admired the beauty all around him. He gazed at the rocky cliffs, rising from the sea into lofty peaks. Intent to find the river's source, he turned to follow it inland. The more he walked, the more he marvelled. Bright patches of moss draped the riverbanks. Tiny gold and purple flowers blossomed among green carpets of grass. Beneath the ocean there were many kinds of strange and lovely seaweeds, corals, grasses, and flowers, but he had never seen such delicate shapes and colors as these. He guessed that the sweet water of the river was to thank, for no grass or flowers grew beyond the river's reach.

This was the second day on Earth.

A band of butterflies suddenly appeared. At first Dragon Prince mistook them for flowers. He had never seen such fragile creatures. They were as light as air, sporting sunlight on their wings as they fluttered among the flowers. No doubt, he mused, they thought the flowers were creatures like themselves.

Dragon Prince climbed the mountain slope down which the river flowed. Its waters bubbled and gushed, caressing the mossy rocks along the banks. Bushes sprang up among the fresh grasses. Then he came to an abrupt halt. Before him was a sight unlike any he had ever encountered. Leaning against a moss-covered boulder was a young woman. Though her face was turned towards the rock, he could tell she was weeping. Unclad, she was more beautiful than any living creature he had seen before. She was like a newly blossomed flower. Her pale arms were folded beneath her forehead. Her long, lustrous black hair curled and flowed with the river currents. It was Au Co, forced to remain in the lower world because she had tasted the sweet earth. She had wept since nightfall, a span of more than ten years to us.

Dragon Prince did not take another step forward. He stood spellbound, and then he spoke:

> Sun shining brightly
> Sky and sea both blue
> Butterflies flutter
> By a river so new
> Where have you come from?
> Why do you weep alone?

Startled by the sea prince's voice, she stopped crying and looked up. Her eyes opened wide in surprise when she beheld the noble young man. She sat up and wiped her eyes with a lock of hair. Looking straight into his eyes, she answered:

> Bright golden crow
> Fragrant new earth
> As white Lac birds
> We flew below.
> A taste of new earth
> No longer can I fly
> My sisters departed
> I wait alone and cry.
> Lost in a strange land
> My tears become a river.

Au Co explained all that had happened from the moment she pulled back the curtain of cloud to the moment she could no longer fly and was forced to return to earth. Dragon Prince sat down beside her and told her about his own life beneath the sea, where his father reigned. His voice was warm and kind, and whenever he mentioned the golden crow, the blue sky, or the fragrant hills, his eyes sparkled. Together they looked up at the sky and down at the green grasses that covered the riverbanks. Dragon Prince tried to console Au Co by telling her that her sisters would surely return that day or the next, as soon as they found a way to take her back home. They spoke for a long time. The sea prince's joy was so infectious that Au Co was soon talking and laughing as though no misfortune had befallen her.

Holding hands, they strolled down the mountain. Suddenly the sea prince grew alarmed. The river had almost completely drained into the sea. The grasses and flowers at their feet were withering. There were no butterflies in sight. The golden crow poised above their heads and their shadows shortened. It was noon, and the crow's rays were fierce and burning.

Dragon Prince said, "The earth is only green and beautiful when nourished by the sweet water of your tears. There are no trees and flowers growing by the seawater. It seems that land plants cannot thrive on seawater. Let me make some rain from the remaining tears in order to replenish the river."

Au Co did not know what rain was. But before she could ask, the prince climbed down to a tiny stream of water still trickling through the white sands about to empty into the sea. He scooped up some of the water in his hands and took three sips. When he returned to where she stood, he said, "Please sit down over there. I will moisten the earth with this wondrous water. Do not cry out until you see the rain. Look out over the ocean. If you see anything strange, do not worry. Although you are a goddess and I am a dragon, there is nothing to fear between us."

He quickly ran back to the sea. Au Co watched as he joined his palms together like a lotus bud. He dove into the water and quickly disappeared from sight. Within moments black clouds tumbled forth from a churning sea. They piled higher and higher until the blue sky was obscured. They were quite unlike the serene white clouds that drifted in the heavens Au Co knew. The golden crow's light grew fainter until Au Co could barely see what was happening. Suddenly, thunder bellowed from the depths of the sea, and a golden dragon hundreds of feet long burst from the waves. Its marvelous long body twisted gracefully before it disappeared into the black clouds. Lightning flashed across the black sky and then there was a deafening crash.

Frightened, Au Co stood up, but she was unable to see anything. Then, all at once, she felt a pleasant sensation on her skin, something at once wet, ticklish, delicate, and refreshing. Thousands of tiny drops fell onto her body. Rain! Dragon Prince had made rain!

The steady pitter-patter was like the sound of singing. It reminded Au Co of the sea prince's warm and reassuring voice. She lifted her arms to welcome the refreshing drops and then offered her hair and shoulders, her whole body, to the soothing rains. Beneath her feet, young grasses sprang up and the river was soon replenished.

The rain lasted a long while. When nearly all the clouds were gone and bright sunlight streamed forth again, the golden dragon gazed down at the earth. Many new rivers and streams had appeared. Not only did grass grow fresh and green along the riverbanks, but it now covered the hills, mountains, and fields. Flowers—violet, gold, pink, and white—dotted the landscape. The face of the earth glistened in unimaginable beauty. Yet what was even more miraculous to the sea prince as he gazed down from the last clouds was that the outline of the rivers took the very shape of Au Co herself—her long legs stretching to the sea, her hair flowing over all the hills and mountains. Her image was forever imprinted on the green fields of the fresh and lovely earth. Au Co, so beautiful and full of vitality, was herself the fertile heart of the earth.

The golden dragon flew back down to earth, turning again into a handsome young man. In his hand he held a white lotus. He was anxious to see the young goddess again. Indeed, he had fallen in love with her the moment he saw her. Au Co awaited the sea prince's return. His voice, as gentle as the early morning sunlight, had warmed her heart.

ONE HUNDRED EGGS

FROM A HIGH CLIFF, Dragon Prince gazed down over the ocean. To him, nothing could match the beauty of morning by the sea. The pale blue horizon rested on the deep blue expanse. Sun sparkled on the waters. He watched fishermen drag their nets over the sand, while others pushed small boats out into the water. They were robust and handsome men, each wearing a dragon tattoo to ward off sea monsters. Dragon Prince was pleased with the human race. They had inherited the intelligence of goddesses from their mother Au Co and the bravery of dragons from their father.

Dragon Prince had no idea how many months or years had passed according to sea time since he met Goddess Au Co, but seven thousand years had passed on earth. Because she was an immortal, Au Co looked as fresh and beautiful as ever. But in those seven thousand years, many generations of the human race had come and gone. Since the birth of the first humans, Dragon Prince and Au Co had been there to teach and protect them. The people looked to Au Co as their ruler and used the image of the Lac bird as the symbol of their land. They often called Dragon Prince "Lac Dragon."

Seven thousand years. . . . Perhaps according to sea time it had been a mere seven months. Here on land, so much had changed. Dragon Prince reminisced about the first day he set foot on land and how he followed the stream of fresh water to discover Au Co. He remembered the first rainfall he made from her tears. Au Co's sweet tears were the source of life for the trees, grasses, flowers, and all living beings on land. Her tears refreshed both body and spirit. Dragon Prince thought of Au Co as the green earth herself in whose heart flowed endless springs of fresh water.

His union with Au Co was very special. She was beauty and vitality. She was the fertile earth. Not long after they began living together, Au Co laid a large sack of eggs. Had they both been dragons, Dragon Prince would have expected their children to be dragons. But this was a union between a dragon and a goddess. Many months passed before they knew what fruit their love was to bear. Although they lived together in a cave near the top of Long Trang mountain, they placed the egg sack outside in a grassy meadow to accustom their future children to the sky, the earth, and the warmth of the sun.

For nine years, they visited the egg sack daily. They sat together on the moist grass beneath the light of the wild swan or beneath the warm rays of the golden crow, listening quietly to the wind sift through the grasses. They usually communicated in silence, understanding each other perfectly. Dragon Prince knew how Au Co felt just by looking into her eyes. And Au Co understood what Dragon Prince wanted to say by the motions of his arms and hands. His outstretched arms resembled golden dragons in graceful flight.

One morning, as the wind sang through the trees, they reached the meadow to discover the egg sack had grown as large as a small hill, and it began to rip apart. When the warm rays of the golden crow came shining over the mountain, one hundred snow-white eggs began to crack open, and from each one emerged a plump baby. Au Co and Dragon Prince were overcome with joy and surprise. One hundred little boys and girls stretched out rosy arms to be held. Au Co and Dragon Prince carried their children back to the cave and made cozy beds for them out of soft grasses. The babies did not need mother's milk to grow. Together with the fresh air and the natural strength they inherited from their goddess mother and dragon father, they grew as quickly as flowers in the field.

Au Co devoted all her time to the care of her one hundred babies.

She rocked each one in her arms, hardly able to believe the wondrous fruits of love. To be a mother was for her the greatest happiness. She loved the earth. She loved all the plants and creatures. She
loved her new life. Now and again she thought longingly of her sister goddesses, but she was no longer overcome by sadness or regret.
The goddesses did not return—perhaps they had been forbidden.
Although Au Co wished to see them again, she was content with
her life on Earth and considered it her true home.

Dragon Prince's thoughts did not dwell much on his former life
beneath the ocean. He remained on land to create a new life by the
side of Au Co. Their children grew daily in strength and wisdom.
Dragon Prince taught them to call him "Father" and to call Au Co
"Mother." Au Co's daughters often called to her in high, sweet voices,
"Mother, can we climb the hill to gather flowers?"

With Au Co, Dragon Prince created a human language and used
it to name all the things on earth. They named the plants and flowers that flourished on land. They called the dense groves of trees
"forests" and the majestic formations of rocks that grazed the skies
"mountains." They named the golden crow "Sun" and the wild swan
"Moon." They called their one hundred children Mountain, Water,
Forest, Moon, Plum, Pear, Peach, Crystal, and many other beautiful
names. One hundred children, and they never forgot the name of a
single one.

When the children were old enough, Au Co and Dragon Prince
showed them how to gather fruit and how to make stone tools to
hunt in the forests. They helped them weave nets to catch shrimp
and fish in the rivers and sea.

Dragon Prince remembered how a god appeared to Au Co in a
dream one cold winter night. The god held a golden crow that glowed
like fire in his hand. Its warmth comforted Au Co. The god introduced himself as A Nhi and he showed her simple tools made from

stone. Then he said, "When the people are cold, they can call me. I am a child of the sun sent to help them. I live in these stones."

When she woke up, Au Co told this dream to Dragon Prince. They went outside to examine their stone tools, but they didn't notice anything unusual. Suddenly Dragon Prince remembered how he and his sons had seen sparks flying from stones while working with their tools. Dragon Prince struck two stones together and used dry twigs and leaves to start a fire from the sparks that were created. From that time on the people had fire for warmth and cooking.

Dragon Prince taught his children to chop wood and build huts. In the winter Au Co shredded tree bark into thread to weave some simple cloth. With the help of her daughters, everyone soon had clothes to wear. They cut and dried reeds to weave mats with which to cover the cold floors of their huts. The people netted shrimp and fish and hunted game with bows and arrows. What food they didn't eat, they learned to dry and preserve to last the winter.

The work Au Co liked best of all was growing sweet rice. The people fashioned simple stone plows and sowed grains of rice. Where the land was low enough, they dug canals for irrigation. Lac Dragon showed his children how they could stuff sections of bamboo trunk with rice and then cover the bamboo with mud to throw onto hot beds of ashes. When the wet mud had dried and cracked away, they scooped out the rice. Rice prepared in this way was especially delicious.

In all ways, a new and wondrous life flourished on earth. Several thousand years passed. The first children grew old and died, as did their children and grandchildren. Each generation passed the land onto the next. Although humans were half-dragon and half-goddess, they lived only a few hundred years. When they died, their souls departed to the underworld, where, it is said, the living can some-times visit. There were, however, a few children endowed with the same powers as their parents. They were immortal and lived in the high mountains or the deep sea, never growing old.

When children came of age, they could marry. A young woman's parents would bring an offering of salt to a young man's parents to request that a marriage be arranged. If the young man's parents agreed, the young man was sent to live with his bride's family. At the wedding, the bride and groom received sweet rice from everyone in the village. The ceremony itself was simple—bride and groom shared a meal of sweet rice together. After the wedding, they continued to live with the bride's family.

The salt offered to the groom's parents was a symbol of trust and friendship. The sweet rice eaten at the wedding was a symbol of intimacy and fidelity. At large weddings, friends of the families brought cakes made of flour pounded from wild roots. Au Co created all these customs for her children.

Human couples did not lay eggs. Instead, the mother gave birth to one child at a time. Au Co showed mothers how to arrange fresh banana leaves for their babies to sleep on and how to nourish the babies with their own breast milk.

Salt was regarded as precious and essential. Au Co showed her children how to extract a kind of salt from gingerroots. Later, Lac Dragon showed them how they could evaporate sea water to obtain salt. Thanks to salt, the people could cure fish and make fish sauce that kept for long periods of time.

Au Co also taught her children to dance and sing. With the people, she organized special nights of dance and song held around great bonfires. The first musical instruments they invented were drums made by stretching animal skins over hollowed out logs. Young men and women also pounded long sticks against the sides of stone urns used to grind rice. Everyone, young and old, joined these celebrations, donning headdresses and vests made of white feathers and dancing around the fire. Later generations replaced the simple wood and stone drums with copper ones that boomed like thunder.

A sudden cry from shore awoke Lac Dragon from his thoughts. He looked below. Thousands of silver fish glistened in the fishermen's nets. It was a tremendous catch! Then, without warning, Dragon Prince felt a curious twitch in his right arm. He knew that his Emperor Father was calling him to return to the sea palace. It was time. His father wished to hand over the throne to him. It had been a long time since Dragon Prince had made an appearance at the sea palace. With a twinge of regret, Lac Dragon knew he had to leave the land and return to the sea. A gentle hand stroked his shoulder, and he looked up. He did not know how long Au Co had been standing behind him. Her hand rested gently on his shoulder.

She asked, "What are you thinking about so deeply?"

He stood up and clasped her hand, "My father, the Sea Emperor, has just summoned me to return to the sea palace to inherit the throne. I must depart at once, but I will return as soon as the coronation ceremony has taken place."

"May I go with you?" she asked.

"Sky is round and earth is square. Water and fire are different elements. You are a goddess and I am a dragon. Although our union on the land is wondrous, it is not possible for you to travel beneath the sea. I wish you could come, but it isn't possible."

"You are right, my dear. But what about our children? Do humans possess the ability to visit the sea palace?"

Lac Dragon thought a moment and then answered, "Because humans are half-dragon, they should be able to. If a boy and a girl were to go together, they could help each other along the way. I'll return just as soon as I've finished my duties beneath the sea, but if any emergency arises before then, send two of our children down to the sea palace for me. Anyone who holds this will find their way without danger."

Lac Dragon opened his mouth and a bright jadestone popped out. He handed it to Au Co.

"My father is calling. I must leave at once."

He took her hand and together they walked down to the beach. It was noon and the fishermen had returned to their villages for lunch. Dragon Prince gazed at the quiet blue sky. He felt as though seven thousand years had passed as quickly as a dream. He held Au Co's hands in his own and looked into her eyes for a long moment. He leaned down and kissed both her cheeks. Then, with a slight twist of his body, he turned into a little fish and dived into the ocean. Startled, Au Co stood and stared at the water. She called out her husband's dragon name. "Naga! Nagaraja!"

But Lac Dragon was already far away. The only answer to her cries was the steady lapping of the waves.

THE VOYAGE

IT HAD NOT rained in over six months. Streams and rivers, bordered by parched grasses, barely trickled. The rice plants were no more than dry straw. The earth was piteously cracked. People sought refuge in the forests to escape the burning noon heat. No wind blew. The air was thick and still, as if weighted by some heavy burden.

Au Co withdrew to the lofty mountains the day Lac Dragon departed. But when she heard the people's tormented cries, she descended. Distressed to see her children's plight, she knew she had to summon Dragon Prince. He had surely ascended to the throne by now. Why was it taking him so long to return?

She had carefully guarded Lac Dragon's jadestone, which she now entrusted to a young man named Hung, and she instructed him to go down to the sea palace and implore the new Dragon Emperor, her husband, to make rain.

Hung was an intelligent and courageous young man from the village of Hac Trang, which was renowned as a center of rich culture and the home of many bright and talented men and women. In the center of Hac Trang grew a four thousand-year-old tree whose branches pierced the white clouds. Its branches, where many cranes nested, shaded a vast area. Whenever Au Co descended the high mountains to meet with her people, she met them beneath this tree.

Hung was well-loved by the other villagers. Although Au Co selected him to go to the sea palace, she was unable to offer him any directions. She simply gave him the jadestone and said he must find a young woman to accompany him. Hung was fond of a young woman his age named Mi. Besides being charming and graceful, she was sharp-witted and capable. Traveling beneath the ocean with Mi would be most pleasant, but he hesitated to ask her. What if they encountered venomous sea monsters? He could not bear the thought of any harm coming to Mi.

On the path to Mi's house, Hung wondered how he would find the way to the sea palace. Au Co said the jadestone would cause the water to part. But the ocean was so immense, how would he know which direction to go? How long would it take to reach the palace? As he was pondering these things, a voice startled him. "What are you thinking about so hard, Hung?"

Hung looked up. On the path in front of him stood Mi, smiling. She said in a playful voice, "Can it be you are wondering how to reach the sea palace? If so, I can help you, because I know the way."

Hung's eyes opened wide in surprise. "How do you know about my quest? Our Goddess Mother asked me to go only this morning. Who told you?"

Mi took his hand and led him up a nearby hillside. She said, "Let's sit here while I tell you my story from the beginning."

She began, "Yesterday at noon, the heat was so unbearable, I went down to the river to wash my face. As you know, all that is left is a small trickle. Even though the water is muddy, I scooped up a handful and meant to splash my face, when I noticed I'd scooped up a tiny pink fish, no bigger than my little finger. Hung, it was so beautiful. It had shiny scales and tiny gemlike eyes. I didn't rinse my face but carried the little fish home. I placed it in a bowl filled with water and went outside to do my chores.

"Suddenly I heard a loud crash. I ran back into the house and discovered the bowl had fallen from the table and shattered. You wouldn't believe it, Hung, but the fish was now a hundred times larger, the size of your arm. I was certainly surprised, and I took it and placed it in our rain barrel, hoping to keep it alive. This morning when I awoke, I went outside to check on it, and Hung! the fish had grown so much it could barely budge in the barrel. I knew then that it must be a magic fish and I said, 'Let me return you to the river.' But the fish answered, 'No, I can't grow smaller again. My permission to stay on land is up. I can only continue growing larger until I resume my original form. If you want to help me, please carry me down to the ocean. I would be most grateful.'

"I was scared, knowing the fish didn't have much time left, so I picked it up and started to run to the seashore. But my arms soon grew tired and I was forced to stop several times to catch my breath. When at last we reached the sea, the fish said, 'I am a princess from the sea palace. Thank you, my sister, for saving my life. I must admit it was foolish of me to swim up a dry riverbed like that. But now the danger has passed. To show my gratitude I will tell you what has caused the drought and how Her Majesty Au Co has asked someone to go down to the sea palace to summon Dragon Emperor. Although I dare not intrude into the affairs of the elders, I can at least offer you some advice. To reach the sea palace, a traveler must first possess a special jadestone which belongs to Dragon Emperor. Two people must make the journey together—a man and a woman. The shortest route is by the Eastern Sea, but if you go that way you must pass by the Sea Monster's lair. Dragon Emperor does not yet know that this monster has been attacking fishermen. This monster possesses such formidable powers, I dare not oppose it in combat alone. But I can teach you a mantra that will so frighten it, it will allow you to pass without harm. Dragon Emperor taught me this mantra himself, to use in perilous situations.'"

"Did you learn it by heart?" asked an excited Hung.

"Yes," replied Mi, "and I'll teach it to you in a moment. The sea princess also told me that the fates had chosen a certain young man to make the journey and that he must ask a young woman to accompany him. She said the young man was a special friend of mine. She said, 'What I am about to tell you will make you the only person on land who knows the way to the sea palace. The first couple to travel beneath the waves will share a brilliant future together. Remember everything I tell you. Tomorrow at sunrise, proceed at once in the direction of the sun until you reach the seaside. When you hold up Dragon Emperor's precious jadestone, the water will part to reveal a path. After you have traveled a short distance you will no longer be able to see by the light of the sun. At that moment, the jadestone will shine like a lantern to guide your steps. Remember that there should be nothing but golden sand beneath your feet at all times. If you step on a stone, a patch of seaweed, or a spot of mud, you will know that you have strayed from the path. Stop at once. Hold the stone up and look around you. Make your way back to the path of golden sand. Do not stray in any direction where you see violet, green, or red. Those colors are a sign that you are near a sea monster's lair.

"After a day's travel, you will begin to notice a natural light again. This will be the light that shines from the crystal sea palace. From then on, you will encounter many kinds of sea creatures, all of whom live under the rule and protection of Dragon Emperor. If you see any beings with long, winding necks, don't be alarmed. Just announce, 'I am a messenger being sent to Nagaraja,' and you will not be hindered from continuing on your way. At Dragon Emperor's palace, you will not encounter any guards since everyone knows well enough not to disturb him during his hours of meditation and work. You may freely enter and announce your arrival. If Dragon Emperor is free to meet you, he will appear in person."

Mi stopped a moment to catch her breath and then continued, "That's not all. The sea princess also said, 'Before you go you must find a spring of fresh water to fill a jug. Our Dragon Father will need that water to make rain. There is a chamber of clouds beneath the sea. Dragon Emperor holds the only key. He cannot make rain good for the land unless he has fresh water. The riverbeds are all muddy or dry, but I know of a deep well not far from the shores of the Eastern Sea. The well itself is dry, but beneath it lies a path that leads to a hidden spring. There is still plenty of fresh, clear water gathered there in a large, stone-lined pool. Once you've filled your jug with water, follow the dry stream bed beneath the well. It will lead you straight out to the Eastern Sea without your having to climb back out of the well.'"

Hung thought carefully to himself, "Tomorrow morning I must depart and Mi must accompany me." He repeated everything Mi had said and the expression in her eyes assured him he remembered every detail.

Mi said, "Now for the mantra. I'll recite it so you can learn it, too. We should both know it in case one of us forgets part of it along the way. Here is how it goes:

> Ruler of all that lives
> Above and below in the sea
> Far and wide, all proclaim
> Valiant Lord Naga's fame.
> Monsters all lie in fear
> When the Dragon Lord appears
> *Gate! Paragate!*

They recited the mantra several times until Hung was certain he knew it by heart. They promised to meet each other the next morning by the village gate when the morning mist was just beginning to lift.

That night Mi told her mother the whole story. Her mother listened intently, now and again clucking her tongue in worry. When Mi finished, her mother went to an old chest that held the family's most treasured belongings. She took out a small vial containing a dozen or so tablets that resembled small white beans. She told Mi, "This is a magic herbal medicine which Goddess Au Co gave to grandmother long ago. Our Goddess Mother gathered the herbs herself in the high mountains to make this remedy. That was in the days when she came down to visit the people more frequently than she does now. Grandmother used this medicine to heal me once when I was at death's door. You have been chosen to go with Hung. It may be a journey fraught with danger, but the people's life depends on it. Take this remedy with you. Keep it securely tucked in your pocket. You and Hung may have need of it."

Mi and her mother talked late into the night. Finally her mother insisted Mi get some rest to be prepared for her journey.

When Mi met Hung at daybreak, she first asked him whether or not he remembered the mantra. He nodded. He was carrying a jug fashioned from a gourd and had a coil of sturdy rope slung over his shoulder. Silently they walked in the morning mist. Leaves crackled beneath their feet and Hung sighed as he looked out over the wasted rice fields. If their quest was a success, a terrible famine could be averted. Some families had already abandoned the village to migrate north in hopes of finding cooler regions less affected by the drought. Mi's own family was making preparations to move. Hung doubted they would find better conditions. There was little hope of finding new lakes large enough to irrigate fields of rice and vegetables. His family was determined to remain and to live or die on their ancestral land. If Mi's family moved, she would have to follow them, and Hung was afraid he might never see her again. In fact, Hung had confided to Mi that he hoped her family would ask for him in marriage.

Hung and Mi reached the well the sea princess had described. Mi peered down the well, but it was too dark to make anything out. Hung shook his head in a gesture of concern. He uncoiled the rope, secured one end around a tree, and tossed the other end down the well. Grabbing hold of the rope, Hung eased his way down into the black mouth of the well. Mi waited, growing anxious. She shouted his name but heard only her own echo.

Finally she heard Hung's muffled voice, but she could not make out the words. Soon, however, he reappeared. He had hoisted himself up, and he sat on the well's rim. "The well is very deep and dark, but the jadestone casts enough light to see by. Climb onto my back and hold tightly. I'll tie a strip of cloth around us to further secure you."

Mi shut her eyes to lessen her fear and clung tightly to Hung's neck and shoulders as he began to work his way back down the sides of the well. It seemed as though they would never reach the bottom. She opened her eyes and was surprised to see the light cast by the jadestone.

At last they touched ground. Mi climbed off Hung's back and let him rest several minutes. The air around them was dank and stale. Hung held up the jadestone so they could take a look around them. They found a low, narrow entrance to a cave. Hung crawled through first, discovering that it was roomy enough to stand on the other side. Pure white stalagmites and stalactites glimmered in the jadestone's light.

Hung called Mi to join him. They followed a path lined with

stones until they reached a streambed. As the magic fish had counseled, they followed it upstream. The fine sand beneath their feet
grew cooler the farther they walked. They had to climb over several
large rocks before hearing the gurgling of running water. Up ahead
hung a thick curtain of stalactites over a barrier of pale green rocks.
The sand beneath their feet was damp.

Mi waited as Hung climbed the green rocks to take a look at the
other side. "Water!" he shouted. Millions of clear drops dripped from
stalactites into an immense pool. Hung helped Mi climb up. It was
a wondrous sight. Not a ripple stirred on the pool's surface. The
only sound was the gentle pitter-patter of falling drops. As she looked
at this source of hidden, cool water, Mi thought about the scorched
land above. She thought, too, of how Goddess Au Co's tears were
the source of all fresh water. She took the gourd from Hung's back
and dipped it into the water. She capped it and then tied it securely
across Hung's back.

Together they climbed back down the barrier of green rocks and
retraced their steps down the streambed. Love filled their hearts as
they skipped along the sand. They passed the well and followed the
streambed that would lead out to the Eastern Sea. Because the path
had been the heart of a stream, the sand was soft and they could
walk easily. But before long, rocks jutted along the path until they
were so thick it was impossible to make out a proper path at all.
Hung and Mi were forced to climb over boulders.

A terrible stench suddenly made Mi stop in her tracks. She looked
at Hung to see if he had noticed anything. He cried out, "What a
terrible smell!"

Mi screamed. Beneath her feet were the skeletal remains of a human.
Human bones lay strewn all about. Hung grabbed her arm. "We must
be near the sea monster's den. Remain calm. Do you remember
the mantra?"

Mi nodded. Though she was frightened, the mantra was secure in her memory. Trying not to make a sound, they made their way forward. A dim light filtered over the rocks, and they could make out the sound of the tides. They were within reach of the Eastern Sea.

Without warning, the sea monster appeared from behind a giant boulder, clutching a fisherman in its jaws. The monster was taller than the haystack outside Mi's house and at least fifty feet long. It was covered with black and white scales. Its forbidding tail lashed back and forth like a whip. Hung let go of Mi's arm and motioned for her to move back. With all the strength he could muster, he jumped against the monster's throat. The sudden blow caused the monster to drop the fisherman. It lunged at Hung, opening its mouth to reveal two rows of dagger-sharp teeth. Hung jumped out of the way in the nick of time.

"Mi! Recite the mantra!"

Hung knew he could not possibly match the monster's strength. The most he could do was to try to avoid the lethal thrashes of its tail and its sharp teeth. After jumping out of the way for the fourth time, he heard Mi's voice rising clear and strong in the cave:

> Ruler of all that lives
> Above and below in the sea
> Far and wide, all proclaim
> Valiant Lord Naga's fame.

The monster looked about as if confused. Seeing the monster's hesitation, Hung bellowed the last lines of the mantra himself:

> Monsters all lie in fear
> When the Dragon Lord appears
> *Gate! Paragate!*

"*Gate! Paragate!*" echoed in the cave like thunder. The sea monster fled in the direction from which it had come, disappearing from sight. The mantra worked.

Hung and Mi ran to see if the fisherman was still alive. The dragon tattoo on his chest had not been enough to ward off the monster. He was covered with bloody tooth marks, but he was breathing. Mi took out the vial of Au Co's remedy. A sweet, refreshing fragrance filled the cave when she uncapped the vial. She placed one of the tablets in the man's mouth and asked him to swallow it. Instantly, every wound disappeared. He stood and opened his mouth but he was too overcome with emotion to speak.

Hung said, "Please, sir, we are not gods. We are ordinary folks like yourself. Please do not feel any need to thank us. We've been asked by Goddess Au Co to go down to the sea palace and ask Lord Naga to return to make rain. We knew, no matter what, that we would have to confront the sea monster. Thank goodness we were in time to save you. For that we're most grateful."

At first it appeared that the only way out of the cave was the same route by which the sea monster had fled. Reluctant to take that route, they searched until they found another way out by climbing over some boulders. Hung and Mi were relieved to breathe the fresh morning air again. They turned towards the Eastern Sea and saw that the sun had already risen past the morning star. They had hoped to be on their way earlier and were now anxious to begin the journey. Hung pointed the way back to the village and said to the fisherman, "Sir, please tell our people to stop fishing near here, and please let them know that messengers have been sent to the sea palace to ask for Lord Naga's help. When Lord Naga returns, he'll undoubtedly take care of the monster. I'm sure you can return to the village without fear. The monster was terrified by the mantra, and I'm sure he won't come back soon."

They bade farewell to the fisherman and walked to the water's edge. Facing the sun, Hung held up the bright jadestone, and the water parted, revealing a wide, golden path. As they descended, the water closed over their heads. The fisherman stood on some high rocks and witnessed this incredible scene. His mouth hung open in astonishment. Since the sea monster dropped him from its terrible jaws and the young woman revived him with the magic remedy, he had been too overcome with shock and gratitude to utter any sound. He climbed down from the rocks and returned to the village, marvelling that he was still alive.

The sun was soon obscured from sight, but the jadestone illuminated the way. Seawater, clear as crystal, continued to part before them, revealing a path of golden sand. They found themselves surrounded by a pocket of air so they could breathe. The water overhead was deep blue but other currents swirled around them—some red as blood, some violet, some pure white.

The path was easy to follow, and neither Hung nor Mi feared losing their way. Nonetheless, they were careful not to stray from the path. They did not relish the idea of meeting up with another sea monster. After some time, Mi grew weary. Her steps slowed and she had to lean on Hung to continue. Finally, Hung suggested they stop for a rest.

Even after resting a long moment, Mi found she had little strength. Hung carried her on his back for a good distance, before he too grew weary. Mi recounted stories she'd heard from her grandmother to help them forget their fatigue. Suddenly, she remembered the vial of Au Co's remedy. She reached into her pocket and uncapped the vial. Just smelling the sweet scent of mountain herbs was refreshing. She took one tablet for herself and gave one to Hung. Their strength was not only instantly restored, but multiplied. They continued on their way with renewed vigor.

They covered a good distance in a short time. The path now led

downhill, quickening their steps. Golden sand seemed to stretch endlessly before them, until all of a sudden, it disappeared. Unable to
explain it, they looked in all directions but saw only sand the hue of
emeralds. They couldn't imagine how they had strayed from the path.
Suddenly, Mi heard a girl's voice by her ear which said, "Follow me."

Startled, Mi looked around but saw no one. The same voice giggled and said, "I'm right in front of you, sister. Can't you see me?"

Then Mi noticed the tiny pink fish, no bigger than her little finger, swimming in front of her. Mi was greatly relieved to recognize
her friend, the magic fish. "I'm afraid we've lost our way. Can you
help us?"

The little fish swam before them to lead the way through crystal
clear water. Light emanating from the nearby sea palace was so bright,
they no longer needed the jadestone. It was as bright as noon on
land. Hung and Mi marvelled at the strange beauty surrounding
them—corals of every shape and shade and plants whose milk-col-
ored tendrils caressed schools of rainbow fish. Bright green grasses,
ten to twelve feet high, swayed in the currents like willows moved
by a tender breeze. They saw exquisite sea roses unlike any rose
they'd ever seen on land. They followed a crystal path bordered by
snow-white pebbles and exotic flowers.

"My poor brother and sister!" exclaimed the little fish. "You've
come all this way burdened by an air bubble. As soon as we reach
the palace, I'll give you a special pill to enable you to breathe in the
water like the rest of us."

They passed through several crystal gates guarded by fierce creatures. Because the sea princess led the way, no one questioned them.
Dragon Emperor's guards were well equipped with natural weapons.
Some had long arms covered with stinging rays, others had ten-foot
jagged swords jutting from their noses. But most of the sea creatures they encountered were not so threatening. Hung and Mi saw

hundreds of mild, graceful fishes who appeared incapable of even wishing harm to another. Fishes puckered their mouths in conversation with one another, but Hung and Mi could not understand their language.

They also saw dragons who twisted their long silver and blue bodies in a most gentle fashion. Some of the younger dragons stared at the dragon tattoo on Hung's chest and eyed him with great curiosity. Some swam up close to him and then quickly retreated to stare at him from a distance. Their mouths seemed curled up in a perpetual smile.

Mi said, "I think they're laughing at us, Hung."

"No, I don't think so. The mouths of dragons just look that way."

In fact, the only one laughing was the kind sea princess who led the way, as she listened to their puzzled conversation. She turned around and said, "We've reached the entrance to Dragon Emperor's palace. Just beyond the crystal courtyard over there, you'll find three large portals. Pass through them and across another wide courtyard in which the sea's most precious plants grow. After you cross the courtyard, you will enter the palace proper. I dare not go with you, for unless I am summoned, I have no right to enter. I'll wait for you here."

Then the fish surprised them by turning into a beautiful young woman. Her strands of long black hair undulated in the water. Sparkles of green light reflecting off the sea palace danced on her pale skin. Instead of legs, she had a large fishtail that swayed gently back and forth. Mi was relieved to see the princess did not have legs, for she might have considered her a rival otherwise. The princess guessed Mi's thoughts and smiled at her knowingly. Mi blushed, embarrassed by her thoughts. The sea princess only smiled again and said, "I can change my tail into legs, as well, but that would not be very practical for sea travel. Here, swallow this remedy and you'll no longer require that cumbersome air bubble. You will also be given tails like mine so you can move about more easily. When you want your legs back, just take out the emperor's jadestone. Your tails will vanish and the air bubble will surround you once more. But don't tarry. I wish you the best of luck."

Mi and Hung swallowed the small pills the princess handed them. The air bubble vanished and in place of legs, they now had fishtails. They found they could glide through the water as effortlessly and rapidly as though they had been born that way. They nodded a fond farewell to the princess and passed through the three portals. In a flash they reached the courtyard of precious plants and then they found themselves in Dragon Emperor's quiet, imposing palace.

Mi looked up. The ceiling was concealed by fog and mist. Jade pillars towered so high she could not tell where they ended. The floor of the huge room was tiled with coral, agate, pearls, and amber. Seaweed twined gracefully up the crystal walls. They passed through several more grand rooms, each enveloped in silence. Finally they reached a large, impressive room which they guessed marked the palace center. An ornate jade throne, larger than Mi's house, sat in the center of the room. But Dragon Emperor was not upon it.

Mi looked at Hung. He approached the throne and spoke respectfully:

Earth groans and cries
One by one, the rivers dry
Your children come before the throne
Please, Father, make your presence known.

His clear voice echoed against the crystal walls. There was a sudden sound like wind blowing, but then all fell silent again. Hung looked at Mi, and she, likewise, stood before the throne. She lifted her voice and spoke from her heart:

Lac Dragon whom we all revere
To your children lend an ear
Goddess Au Co hopes and waits
On you depends your children's fate
Sent by Mother, we are here
Please, our Father, lend your ear.

They heard a deep sigh that grew into the sound of a strong gale.
The palace shook and, all at once, Dragon Emperor sat before them.

He had a long, white beard and rosy cheeks. His eyes twinkled. An imperial symbol was emblazoned on his broad chest, encrusted with gems, agate, and amber. He towered over them, but Hung and Mi were not at all afraid. His expression was kind, and he appeared somewhat puzzled.

Seeing his confusion, Mi motioned to Hung to take out the jade-stone. Their tails turned back to legs and once again they were surrounded by a bubble of air. Dragon Emperor smiled and said, "When I heard your voices, I knew that two of my land children were here. I was surprised to see you swimming like sea creatures. But I can see you carry my jadestone, the one I gave to Au Co. What brings you here, my children?"

Hung and Mi recounted everything that had taken place since his departure—the tragic drought, the sea monster attacking fishermen, villagers migrating north in search of water. They told him of their journey beneath the sea and how the sea princess had offered them a special remedy. Dragon Emperor laughed,

"So my little daughter has played a part in all this!"

He took them both by the hand and escorted them around the palace. They passed through high portals into magnificent rooms until they reached an enormous reception hall filled with sofas and chairs. Dragon Emperor invited them to sit down beside him on a couch.

"Here, drink this, my children," he said, handing them cups filled with a fragrant liquid. "This special nectar is distilled from precious sea flowers and fruits. It will restore your strength."

They raised their cups respectfully before sipping the nectar. It was no less wondrous than Goddess Au Co's herbal tablets. They felt wonderfully refreshed.

"The coronation kept me very busy," began Dragon Emperor. "I'm afraid I forgot how different time on land is from time here. You children belong to the seventy-second generation of land people.

Because your mother is a goddess and I am a dragon, we are immortal. I sometimes forget how quickly time passes for our mortal children, and thus the people have suffered terribly in my absence. After the coronation ceremony, I retired for a quick snatch of sleep. Imagine that a sea nap lasted six months according to land time! I gave strict instructions to my daughter not to awaken me unless there was a matter of great urgency. But you've already met Sita, the dragon princess, haven't you? Why didn't she come and awaken me herself?"

He boomed, "Sita, child!"

The princess didn't wait to be called a second time. She appeared instantly as a young woman with two perfect legs. She sat down on the couch next to Mi and smiled. Mi smiled back. She was glad to see the sea princess again.

"I didn't come to awaken you myself, Father, because you told me to summon you only if there was an urgent matter concerning any of the sea creatures. Anyway, I knew that my sister Mi's voice could awaken you."

Dragon Emperor smiled and said, "Listen, my children, we must make rain at once. I don't have any fresh water down here so we'll first have to return to land for some. Surely we can find some hidden spring deep in the earth."

Mi untied the gourd of fresh water from Hung's back and handed it to Dragon Emperor, who nodded his approval. He took three swallows of the water and said, "Follow me, children, into the cloud chamber."

The cloud chamber was a huge room whose jade pillars were cloaked in fog. Dragon Emperor whispered a mantra, whereupon a thin stream of water issued from his lips and curled up into the clouds that formed the chamber's ceiling. With a wave of his hand, Dragon Emperor parted the ceiling to allow clouds to tumble out of the palace and burst forth from the sea.

Then he held out his great arm and told his three children to hold on tightly as he lifted them up onto the surface of the ocean. He tossed one of his slippers onto the waves, and it turned into a boat into which they all climbed. Black storm clouds obscured the sun. Thunder boomed and lightning streaked. Dragon Emperor disappeared from the boat. The clouds shook violently. With a mighty clap of thunder, torrents of rain began to fall.

When Dragon Emperor joined them again, he was dressed in the simple garb of a fisherman. All of them were soon soaked by the rains as he steered the boat toward shore. The rain didn't stop until shortly before they reached the shore. Dragon Emperor assured them that this had been enough rain to revive the land.

Hung and Mi knew they were quite near the sea monster's lair. Sudden waves crashed against their small craft and a terrible stench filled the air. Dragon Emperor recited another mantra to calm the waves. Hung was startled to see how drastically the area surrounding the monster's den had changed since that morning. Boulders the size of houses had fallen from the cliffs, forming a nearly completed barrier to prevent the monster from entering the cove. Hung wondered whose strong arms could have shoved such massive boulders off the cliffs in a day's time. Perhaps Mother Au Co had been able to summon gods from above? Hung did not have more time to wonder, for at that instant the monster made its gruesome appearance. It had grown since the morning. Legs now covered its body like a centipede's. Its horrid, gaping mouth revealed rows of dagger-sharp teeth. Its tail thrashed as it prepared to attack. Dragon Emperor, disguised as a simple fisherman, calmly steered the boat right toward the monster.

When they were almost upon it, Dragon Emperor stood up. He put his arms around Sita and pushed her into the wide open jaws of the monster. The princess showed no sign of fear. To Hung and

Mi's astonishment, she turned into a red hot fireball, the size of a copper drum. The monster, its insides seared by the fireball, shrieked and lunged forward. Dragon Emperor stretched to several times his height, drew his sword, and chopped off the monster's tail. Realizing that this was no simple fisherman but Dragon Emperor himself, the monster turned itself into a seal and made a desperate attempt to escape beneath the waves. But Dragon Emperor hurled a huge boulder into the water and forced the monster back to the surface. He cut off its head and flung both head and tail against the cliffs. The rest of the monster's body drifted slowly out to sea.

Then Dragon Emperor guided their boat to shore. Off in the distance, the rice fields were already fresh and green from the rains. Soft grasses covered the hills. The sounds of flutes, drums, and bells drifted toward them. They followed the sound of the music and found the streets crowded with children, who were decked out in handsome new clothes, as were all of the village's adults. Sticks of incense were lit all along the pathways, and the pungent scent of sandalwood filled the air. Mi asked a young mother who was watching her two children dance on the fresh grass what all the celebrating was about.

"Today is the day of Dragon Emperor's return! The people are gathering to greet him. Early this morning, Goddess Au Co sent two messengers to the sea palace. At noon there was rain! We are sure Dragon Emperor will pass by here. Run and join the festivities over there on the hill!"

The woman pointed to a nearby hill where they could see a great throng of people gathering. The air vibrated with singing and drums. Mi thanked the woman and they followed the path up the hill. Sita was very excited. She exclaimed, "What fun it is here on land!"

Dragon Emperor said, "We can't stay long, for I'm afraid once the people realize who Hung and Mi are, we'll be obliged to stay the whole night! We should return Hung and Mi to their own village where their families anxiously await their safe return. But you can join the festivities for a little while."

Dragon Emperor smiled and touched each of them gently on the head. To their surprise, they were transformed into three young children. A perfect disguise! They followed their fisherman father to join the happy crowds. They watched dancers with bright copper bracelets encircling their wrists and ankles dance to the bellowing drums. Long tables were laden with jugs of sweet rice wine. On a center stage decorated with palm leaves was a large coral dragon and a Lac bird made from white feathers. Everything delighted Princess Sita.

When dusk began to fall, they departed. On the path to Hac Trang, the fields were greener than ever. Hung and Mi could not conceal their joy. Dragon Emperor gazed out over the land and looked at each of his children. He was content once more to don the simple clothes of a fisherman.

CUSTOMS AND CULTURE

THE ARECA TREE

TAN AND LANG were brothers. Though Tan was a year older than Lang, they were as alike in looks as two drops of water. No one could tell them apart. No one, that is, except the lovely Thao, whose father taught the village youth. During their years of studies together, Tan, Lang, and Thao became the best of friends.

At first Thao could not distinguish between the two brothers. They wore identical clothes and their hair was cut the same way. Then one stormy night when the brothers stayed late at their teacher's home, Thao saw her chance. She prepared rice porridge for their meal and brought out one bowl and one pair of chopsticks and placed them on the table between the two brothers. She returned to the kitchen and watched them through a crack in the door. One brother motioned to the other to eat first, a privilege reserved for an elder brother. Now Thao knew which brother was Tan. She quickly brought out a second bowl for Lang. All evening, she observed the brothers carefully, until she managed to discover one small differ-ence between them. Lang had a tiny mole on his right ear.

After that, her father and classmates were impressed by Thao's ability to tell the brothers apart. She never handed Tan's notebook to Lang, and she always greeted each brother by his own name. Over time, Thao noticed differences in the brothers' personalities. Tan was outgoing and talkative. Lang tended to be quiet and pensive. Gradually, she could tell them apart merely by looking into their eyes. And although their voices were similar, she was sensitive enough to hear each boy's nature expressed in his words.

One New Year's Day the two brothers came to offer their respects to Thao's father. Suddenly Thao realized that Tan was in love with her. She couldn't explain exactly why, but the look in his eyes let her know beyond the shadow of a doubt. And as for Lang? Thao was so shaken by Tan's look, she did not notice Lang's.

Not long afterwards, Tan's parents brought the traditional offering of salt to Thao's parents to ask for her hand in marriage to their elder son. Thao's parents agreed. With some regret, Thao left the home of her parents to go live with her husband's family. She wished that her people still followed the old custom of having the groom live with the bride's family. But she loved Tan and was happy to be his wife. On their wedding day, Tan wore a robe the cheerful color of green banana shoots. Lang's robe was a deep shade of violet.

Each day, Thao saw how deeply her husband loved his younger brother. When she and Tan strolled beneath the moonlight, drank tea, went horseback riding, or played chess, Tan always invited Lang to join them. In fact, Lang wanted the couple to enjoy time alone, but Tan insisted on Lang's presence. Lang pretended to enjoy these occasions, while deep down he longed for more solitude. He found great contentment spending quiet moments on his own. Tan was unable to understand this need in his brother and could not bear the thought of Lang being left alone. Thao tried to speak to Tan about Lang's special needs, but Tan would not listen.

A new discovery added to Thao's concern. Lang was also in love with her. Love burned within him like a fiery volcano. Although he appeared cool and indifferent on the outside, Thao was sensitive enough to know the truth.

One day Lang told them he wanted to retire to a remote mountain hut where he could tend a garden and compose poems. Thao hoped her husband would support Lang's idea, but instead he insisted Lang remain with them.

One dark evening when the brothers returned from a day's labor in the rice fields, Thao mistook Lang for her husband when he entered their hut first. She opened her arms to greet him. Lang hastily removed himself from her embrace and Thao realized her error.

The next morning as they shared rice porridge, Lang informed Tan and Thao that he was taking the day off. Though he laughed as he spoke, Thao detected his anguish. She loved her husband, but that did not prevent her from feeling Lang's pain.

Lang did not return that evening. Ten days passed and there was still no word from him. Frantic, Tan left home to search for his brother. Ten more days passed and neither brother had returned. Thao was beside herself with worry. She left home herself to look for Tan. Like both brothers she followed the road that led out of the capital city's southern gate. There the road forked. One side led up into the mountains, the other down to the sea. She chose the mountain route.

Thao walked for days until her sandals were no more than shreds and her feet were swollen and bloody. Matted locks of hair fell into her eyes. All she had left was a straw hat to protect her from the sun. She felt almost too weak to continue. Her heart was filled with dread.

Somehow she knew that Tan and Lang had passed by this same way, and that knowledge alone kept her going. She tore strips of cloth from her shirt to wrap her blistered feet and trudged on until she came to the banks of a wide river. It was evening, and there was no ferry in sight. A slight wind rustled overhead leaves, and a few birds called in shrill voices. Thao was prepared to spend the night by the river, when she noticed a tiny hut perched on stilts a couple hundred yards away on her side of the shore. A sudden gust of wind sent dry leaves flying. Black clouds gathered at the horizon. Thao knew a storm was brewing. She made her way to the hut and climbed up the ladder to knock on the door. She was greeted, somewhat cautiously, by a woman who looked at her oddly but then urged her to enter. She took Thao's hat and invited her to be seated on a low bamboo bench. Dinner was spread out on a simple mat. Thao greeted the woman's husband, who was feeding their baby spoonfuls of rice.

The woman took out an extra bowl and chopsticks for Thao but Thao politely declined. She was too exhausted to eat but gladly accepted a bowl of hot tea. There was a sudden crash of thunder outside. Wind howled and rain beat against the hut. The sounds of the storm momentarily quieted the storm raging in Thao's own heart. The highland farmer lit a small lamp which cast a dim light. His wife put their child to bed in the next room, the strains of her lullaby drowned out by the raging storm.

When the baby was asleep, the woman rejoined them. Thao asked the couple, "Have you, by any chance, seen a young man in a green robe pass by this way recently?"

Neither the man nor his wife spoke. The man looked at Thao with a strange expression.

Frightened, Thao asked, "Has something happened? Have you seen him then?"

The man slowly answered, "Yes, we did see such a man. What's more, we saw another man who looked just like him but was dressed in white. But I don't think you'll be finding either of them now. Please spend the night with us. You can't go out again in this storm. Tomorrow you can return safely home."

A chill ran down Thao's spine. A feeling of doom closed in around her, as she listened to the woman speak. "Move in a little closer so you can escape the draft that sneaks in by the door. I'll tell you every-thing we know.

"One afternoon, about a month ago, I saw a man dressed in white approach the river. He was empty handed and didn't have even a hat or jacket. My husband was still working in the fields. I wanted to run out and tell the man that he had just missed the last ferry of the day, but I was occupied with the baby and couldn't go out right then. The man looked as if he was searching for something. It was odd, Miss, how he looked up at the sky and down at the ground. He turned his head this way and that before sitting down on the riverbank and holding his face in his hands. He began to shake and I could tell he was weeping. I felt uneasy and wanted my husband to hurry home so he could invite the poor fellow up to our hut. It began to rain lightly, and the man raised his head to the sky again. Then I thought he saw something, because he stretched out his arms as if to embrace someone. But, Miss, all he embraced was the empty air. The rain started coming down harder and soon I could not make him out very clearly. When my husband returned from the fields, I handed him a rain jacket and asked him to go down and fetch the fellow."

The highland farmer took a long sip of tea and said, "I found him sitting like a stone down by the riverbank, not flinching a muscle in all that wind and rain. I asked him several times to put on the jacket and join us inside, but he only shook his head. Finally, I left the jacket on the ground beside him and returned alone. The rain was really pouring by then."

"It was a storm like tonight," said the woman. "We couldn't fall asleep thinking about that poor fellow. All we could hope was that he'd get up out of the rain and return to his home. At dawn, all that was left of the storm was a light drizzle. I looked out the door and thought I saw the man still sitting by the riverbank. I put on a jacket and made my way out. Imagine my surprise when I realized it wasn't the man at all but a large white rock. Next to the rock was the rain jacket my husband had left the night before."

The man spoke, "It was so strange, Miss. That pure white rock hadn't ever been there before. We don't see any rocks like that up in these parts. It seemed unlikely that the man had dragged it there in the night. Anyway, I don't think four men could have budged a stone that size. Rocks don't just spring up out of the earth overnight. We couldn't figure it out. As for the man, we guessed he'd returned the way he'd come or perhaps even thrown himself into the river. That's what my wife thought, anyway, but I couldn't imagine what would drive a man to such desperate measures."

The farmer lit his pipe and took a long, thoughtful puff. His wife continued, "Ten days later another man dressed in green came. He looked all around him, too, like he was lost. Then he came up to our house and asked if we'd seen the other man dressed in white. When my husband told him all we'd seen, his eyes filled with tears. He cried out, 'My brother has turned to stone!' He ran to the river to find the rock just as it was beginning to rain. We had another storm and, though we tried to convince the man to come inside, he refused to budge from the rock. He leaned against it and wept bitterly. Once again, my husband and I spent a sleepless night. In the morning, when we went outside, we didn't see the man, but there was a tree of the palm family, tall as a ten-year-old child, growing beside the rock. That tree hadn't been there before. What kind of tree grows that fast? I told my husband that the man dressed in green must have turned into the tree and that the rock was the man dressed in white. I believe the two men were brothers who loved each other deeply. Some terrible sorrow or misunderstanding must have taken place between them. But you, Miss, are you related to those men? Why are you looking for them? It's another stormy night. Please don't think of going out again. Stay with us tonight, I implore you."

Thao wiped tears from her eyes and made an effort to smile. To ease the mountain couple, she pretended to make light of the whole affair, "Don't worry about me. I'm the housekeeper of the man dressed in green. The man dressed in white is my master's younger brother. I'm sure they simply crossed the river early in the morning after the storms. I'll be crossing the river tomorrow myself. I'm sure I'll find them. I doubt they've gone too far. Please don't worry—I have no intention of venturing out in this storm tonight. I'd be grateful to spend the night here and then I'll catch the first ferry in the morning."

Having reassured them, Thao asked for a mat to serve as a blanket and, after the couple retired to the back room, she lay down. Wind shrieked and battered at the walls as Thao's tears soaked her mat. The lamp's wick cast a bare flicker of light that trembled in the cold drafts seeping in through the doorway. A deafening clap of thunder made Thao wonder if heaven and earth had been reduced to dust.

The storm's fury seemed endless. But at long last, the winds died down. Shortly before dawn, all was quiet. Thao rose, careful not to make a sound. She opened the door and climbed down the ladder. A bright moon emerged from wisps of cloud. By its light, Thao could easily make out the white rock by the shore. Slowly she walked towards it.

It was just as the kind couple had described. A tree with bright green leaves and trunk stood by the rock, slightly bending over as if to protect it. Thao knelt by the rock and put her arms around the tree. She hid her face in its leaves and wept. Some of her warm tears

fell on the rock and seemed to sizzle. Clinging to the tree, her knees
sank into the soft, muddy earth.

When the couple awoke, the young woman was gone. They went
down to shore and asked the ferryman if he had carried her across

the river. He replied, "No, this is my first trip of the day. I haven't carried anyone across yet."

They asked if days before he had carried a man dressed in green or a man dressed in white. Again the answer was no. The couple walked to the white rock. The tree had grown a good two feet in the night and clinging to it was a fresh, green vine. The roots of the vine began deep beneath the rock which it stretched across before twining gracefully up the tree. It almost seemed to be supporting the tree to stand upright. They plucked a vine leaf and crumbled it. It gave an ardent fragrance which reminded them of the young woman whose gaze had been so deep the night before.

* * * * *

One summer afternoon, a party on horseback, led by King Hung Vuong II, came to rest along the riverbank. They noticed a small shrine sheltered beneath several large trees. King Hung dismounted close to the shrine. There he sat down on a smooth white rock while fanning himself. An attendant offered to wave the fan for him, but the king shook his head and smiled. He pointed to the tall straight trees around them and asked the attendant, "What kind of trees are these? The upper branches are laden with fruit. And do you know whose shrine this is?"

The attendant did not know, but seeing the king's curiosity, he climbed one of the trees and picked two of the fruits. Another attendant standing nearby said, "Your majesty, I do not know the name of these trees or fruit, but I do know something about their origin and why the shrine is here."

He told the king the story of Tan, Lang, and Thao as though he had once heard it in detail from the mountain couple.

"Your majesty, the white rock you are sitting on is the kind of rock

Lang turned into. The fruit in your hand comes from the kind of tree Tan turned into. And the green vines that you see twining around the trees are like the vine Thao became. People in these parts say that the white rock represents Lang's pure heart. The tall, straight trees that shade the rocks represent Tan's desire to protect his younger brother, and the graceful vine shows the spirit of Thao who even after death remains at her husband's side. When the parents of these young people came looking for them, the farmer and his wife explained what had happened. The two families had this shrine built. Since then, local people have continued to light incense here to honor the memory of Tan, Lang, and Thao."

King Hung regarded the fruit in his hand for a long moment. He looked at the trees and vines and gently patted the white rock as though it were a small child. He was deeply moved by the story. He handed the fruit to his attendant and said, "Please cut this fruit so I might taste it."

The attendant took out a knife, peeled the fruit, and cut it into eight sections. Each slice of the white fruit held a portion of a smooth pink seed. The king placed a slice in his mouth. It was not sweet like a guava but had a special tang he found refreshing. He crumbled a vine leaf and chewed it along with the fruit. The combined taste was even better. His mouth watered and he spat. A few drops of his saliva fell on the white rock and turned as red as blood. The king put a finger in his mouth and pulled it out but there was no trace of red on it. He asked his attendant to scrape off a small chip of rock which he chewed with the fruit and leaf. His lips were soon stained as red as a young maiden's.

He invited his companions to taste a bit of fruit with leaf and rock. They all found the tangy taste most agreeable, and soon their lips were stained red, as well.

King Hung spoke, "The love and bond between two brothers and husband and wife has borne a deep and ardent fruit. I decree that from now on this fruit and leaf and rock will be used in place of the traditional offering of salt for marriage proposals and weddings. They shall be symbols of love and fidelity."

The others bowed to acknowledge the king's decree. Soon after that the trees and vines were planted throughout the kingdom. The trees were named "Cao" after Tan and Lang's family name, and the vine was called "Lu" after Thao's family name. Thus the custom of chewing areca wrapped in a betel leaf with a sliver of quicklime began among the people.

EARTH CAKES, SKY CAKES

TET, the New Year, had arrived. All the king's relatives and friends had been invited to the palace to watch him wrap earth and sky cakes.

King Hung Vuong II was a just and good-hearted king. His joyful spirit attracted wholesome and talented people to help him run the country. Many people who had committed crimes repented and became fine citizens thanks to his great mercy. He wrote laws and created new customs to enhance the lives of the people. It was thanks to King Hung Vuong II that the people of Van Lang chewed areca, a custom that warmed the atmosphere at all social gatherings.

For several years, people throughout the kingdom had imitated King Hung in making earth and sky cakes to offer the ancestors at Tet. It was said, however, that no one's cakes could compare to the king's, and people wondered if he had some special technique of wrapping them. When the king heard this, he smiled, and then he invited all the court for a New Year's Eve dinner, after which they could watch and help him make the cakes.

Princess Thanh Dung, the king's beloved daughter, greeted the guests as they arrived. She offered the adults a slice of areca and gave the children coconut candy and banana cake that she herself had made. The children, dressed in new clothes, flocked around her like excited small birds.

As areca was chewed, happy conversation popped like corn. Then King Hung entered the hall, and everyone stood silently. He was dressed in a golden robe with a dragon embroidered across the chest, wearing a crown shaped like a Lac bird fashioned from feathers and jade, and his slippers were bright red. The king opened his arms wide and welcomed all his guests, "Please be seated and continue your happy conversations!"

He walked throughout the hall to greet each person individually. Then he sat upon the throne in the center of the hall, and his atten-dants served everyone a simple meal of sweet rice and peanuts. After the guests finished eating, the king's attendants set up a long table in the hall and placed the ingredients for earth and sky cakes—fresh banana leaves, sweet long grain rice already soaked and rinsed, and yellow mung beans—on it. Everyone knew that these were the nec-essary ingredients for New Year's cakes, but how the king made such beautiful cakes was still a mystery to all present.

A fire was built that warmed the hall and on it a huge kettle was placed in which to boil the earth cakes. The king left to change and soon returned wearing simple cotton clothes. Everyone listened intently as he spoke: "My friends, I have invited you here this evening to tell you a story. You all know how to make New Year's cakes to offer our ancestors. Many of you, better cooks than I, make far more delicious cakes than I do. But the most important ingredient, which I hope my story will show, is love."

Then the king told them this story. . .

• • • • •

Though Lieu was a son of King Hung Vuong I, he did not live as luxuriously as the other princes and princesses of the kingdom. His mother, one of the king's consorts, preferred a simple, country life. To her, wealth was unnecessary. She asked for nothing from the king and taught her son to live simply in order to have the time to learn what was truly worthwhile in life.

One day, the king issued a decree that each prince was to prepare a special dish to offer at the ancestral altar on New Year's Day. He said that each offering should express deep respect and gratitude to the ancestors. Because Lieu lived in the country far from the palace, he learned of the decree much later than his brothers. What's more, his mother had recently died and he had no one to counsel him about palace etiquette.

He thought about the king's decree. It was like a competition. The prince who brought the most precious and delicious dish would surely be commended and perhaps even given a high post. Lieu had no money to buy exotic ingredients, nor did he possess great skill as a cook. He felt disturbed. He believed the kingdom flourished because of the virtue and knowledge people possessed and not because they had the wealth to prepare exotic cuisine. He resolved not to enter the contest and took a long walk to try to forget about it. That night he went to bed without supper.

His mother appeared to him in a dream. She smiled kindly and said, "My son, you have misunderstood the king. He does not demand wealth or fancy skill as a cook. He is looking only for a good heart, and that I know you possess."

Lieu wanted to ask his mother what she meant but she only smiled and pointed to the rice fields with one hand and to the sky with the other. When Lieu awoke he thought about his dream. Yes, his mother was surely right. The king was looking for more than exotic food. How could Lieu best express his gratitude and respect to the ancestors? And how could he show his desire to protect all that the ancestors had built? Could he do it without using rare and precious ingredients?

He thought about his mother's clue—one hand pointing to the rice fields and one hand pointing to the blue sky. Of course! The square-shaped paddies were an image of Earth and the blue sky an image of heaven. Earth nourished the people. Heaven watched over them. These were the most precious gifts bequeathed them by their Goddess Mother and Dragon Father.

Lieu sat looking out over the rice fields all morning. At noon he had an idea. He walked back to his hut and soaked a pot of sweet rice after selecting the most perfect grains. He also soaked a pot of beans and then placed them on the fire to cook. He gathered fresh banana leaves in the forest. He planned to make some cakes that were square-shaped to represent Mother Earth and all the plants that flourished on her. He used sweet rice because it was the people's most basic and essential food, enjoyed by even the poorest families in the kingdom.

He filled the cakes with bean paste and fragrant onions to represent other gifts from the earth. He shaped the cakes into perfect squares and wrapped them in fresh banana leaves bound by thin strips of bamboo. He boiled them in a large kettle until the rice was cooked. While the earth cakes were boiling, he steamed another pot of sweet rice which he then pounded into a smooth paste. He shaped the paste into spheres to represent the sky and placed them on fresh green leaves. Both kinds of cakes were made without any waste, using only the simple ingredients that were available to all people, rich or poor.

When the earth cakes were done, he opened one up. The banana leaves had left a faint imprint of green. When he cut the cake open, up rose a familiar and delicious smell. He knew that his square cakes were a worthy symbol of Mother Earth, and his round cakes a worthy symbol of heaven. He selected the ten best of both kinds and put them aside before retiring for the night.

That night his mother visited him again in a dream. She did not speak but her smile told Lieu how pleased she was with the cakes.

In the morning, he put on a clean robe and sandals, and carried the cakes in two baskets balanced on a shoulder yoke. By the time he reached the palace, the other princes had already placed their exotic and fancy dishes on the ancestral altar. Lieu suddenly felt ashamed at how humble his offering was. He feared his brothers would laugh at him. Nonetheless, he placed his cakes on the altar next to the other offerings. The king commenced the New Year ceremonies.

After the ancestral offerings had been made, each prince carried his dish down for the king to examine and taste. The king stood for a long moment in front of each offering and asked each prince in detail about its preparation. Some dishes were made with delicate ingredients which could only be found in the deepest reaches of the forests or upon the highest mountains. Others were cooked from rare ingredients fished from the hearts of rivers or the depths of the sea. The king paused when he reached the earth and sky cakes. He asked Lieu how he had made them and whether their shapes had any meaning. He gazed at Lieu for a long quiet moment. Lieu felt uneasy standing there among his richly clad brothers. The king asked to taste the two cakes and then complimented Lieu on their good flavor. He moved on to carefully examine all the other dishes.

A month later Lieu was summoned to the palace. The king told him that because he possessed the heart, piety, and talent to protect the kingdom and honor the ancestors, the king intended to pass the throne on to him. Lieu was overcome with surprise and asked the king how he had arrived at such a decision. The king told him that the earth and sky cakes had been enough to let him know that Lieu would be a worthy king. That evening the king announced his decision to the people. Not one of the other princes expressed any resentment or jealousy.

And so Lieu, who had been raised in the simple countryside, became King Hung Vuong II. He taught the people how to make earth and sky cakes, telling them that it was not skill in cooking that mattered, but a heart filled with love and gratitude. To this day, Vietnamese families offer such cakes on their ancestral altars at Tet, their hearts filled with love for their homeland.

WATERMELON SEEDS

W HEN AN TIEM was seven years old, he lost both his parents. Because he was a bright and eager child, he was accepted as a sailor's helper on a merchant ship that traded silk, medicines, spices, and sugar from India for sandalwood, anise, cinnamon, and pepper from Vietnam. One day the ship's captain let An Tiem tag along when he went to pay respects to King Hung Vuong III. The king took an immediate liking to the boy, and when he learned he was an orphan, he offered to raise him as his own son.

When An Tiem reached manhood, the king gave him his daughter Oanh in marriage. Because An Tiem was fluent in several languages from his experience aboard the merchant ship, the king placed him in charge of foreign trade. An Tiem quickly acquired great wealth. Profit was not his motive, however. He simply wanted to devote his best efforts to develop trade for the kingdom. Nonetheless, many at court were jealous of him and claimed his success was due only to the king's favor.

One day King Hung summoned An Tiem and said, "An Tiem, some say you are an ungrateful son. They claim you told them that your success is not due to any help from me. Did you say such a thing?"

An Tiem answered, "Father, I am not ungrateful. I know very well that I could not be where I am today without all your generous support. I did say, however, that I enjoy good fruits in this life because of good deeds I did in former lives. When I was a small child, I was taught these lines:

> To know the seeds planted in former lives
> Look at the fruits reaped in this life.
> To know the fruits your future lives hold
> Look at the seeds you now sow.

"I have never forgotten those lines. I believe they speak the truth."

The king asked, "Do you believe then that because of your good deeds in former lives, you were adopted by me in this life?"

"Yes, Father, I do."

King Hung was silent for a moment and then asked, "Well then, suppose I banished you to a deserted island with no one but your wife and young son. Do you think you could survive? If I understand what you've just told me, you should reap good fruits no matter where you are, as long as you have sown good seeds in the past."

"Yes, Father, I believe that to be so."

The king was angered. "Very well, I banish you, your wife, and child to Sa Chau Island. We'll see how well your theory of seeds and fruits holds up."

Resolute, An Tiem answered, "As you wish, Father."

The following day, An Tiem, Oanh, and their six-year-old son Hao, were carried in a small boat to the island. There they were abandoned with only enough food supplies to last a few months. When the sailor who had transported them left for the mainland, Oanh burst into tears.

An Tiem tried to console her by saying, "Don't despair. If we have sown good seeds, we will reap good fruits. If we have sown bad seeds, tears cannot change our situation. Using our hands and wits, we'll find ways to survive. Don't you remember the saying, 'Nature did not create elephants without also creating grass?'"

Placing her faith in her husband, Oanh did not weep again. Together they built a watertight shelter from driftwood and palm fronds. They explored the island in search of edible fruits and greens but found nothing. They had not been allowed to bring along any seeds. But they made their own nets to catch fish and shrimp and collected small flints to start cooking fires. They dried the extra fish and shrimp they netted. They only regretted they had no means to cultivate fruits and vegetables.

By the end of the fourth month of their exile, the food supplies they had brought with them were exhausted. It looked as though they would be forced to live on nothing but fish and shrimp forever. Then one day they discovered a patch of unusual melons growing on the other side of the island. Each fruit was at least three times larger than any melon they had ever seen. When they cut one open, it was ruby red inside with black seeds. To their delight, it was won-derfully sweet. They shared an entire melon beneath the hot sun. It was cool and refreshing and soon lifted their spirits.

An Tiem recalled how several weeks earlier the cries of a flock of cranes flying over the island caused him to look up. He had noticed a few black seeds drop from their beaks but had given it no further thought. Who could have known they were the precious seeds of a new kind of melon? That evening, An Tiem and Oanh prepared a garden patch and planted several of the black seeds.

Just when An Tiem began the first harvest, a foreign ship paid an unexpected visit to the island. Their sails had been damaged in a storm. An Tiem helped them repair the sails and showed them where they could fill their barrels with fresh water. He also picked and sliced one of the melons to offer the sailors. Finding the melon sweet and delicious, they asked An Tiem if they could purchase more. An Tiem traded thirty of the melons for rye, beans, salt, sugar, and cloth. He also told them that if they stopped by the island in another four months, he could provide them with several hundred more melons. In exchange, he asked them to bring grains and other provisions. They agreed.

Four months passed. The new melons were ready to pick. Even if the sailors did not return, An Tiem and Oanh had planted rye and red beans and knew they now had ample means to survive. Oanh sewed them all new garments from the sailors' cloth.

An Tiem named the melon after their son, telling his wife, "This special melon has provided us with a future. Our son is our future, too. So we will call these hao melons." Oanh liked her husband's idea. Although she missed their life on the mainland, she stood by her husband, placing complete faith in him.

An Tiem and Hao went for a stroll along the shore. Suddenly they heard Oanh shouting something from their hut.

"The ship is here! The ship!"

Hao jumped up and looked out over the sea. Sure enough, there was the ship, still no more than a speck. With each minute, it grew larger until it reached shore. An Tiem greeted the sailors and led them to the watermelon patch. Vines laden with jade-green fruit stretched along the fine, sandy soil. They picked a great pile of melons, more than six hundred.

An Tiem exchanged the melons for many kinds of seeds, tools, and other provisions which he and the sailors unloaded and stored safely in a cave on the island.

An Tiem's family continued to cultivate hao melons. The island's sandy soil was ideal, and their crop flourished. The merchant ship began stopping by the island every month to purchase melons to trade at other ports. The sweet red melon was soon in great demand.

It wasn't long before An Tiem was able to build a grand house for his family surrounded by fields of rice and beans. He even raised livestock and hired workers from the mainland.

Four years had passed since they were exiled to Sa Chau Island. One day An Tiem sent twenty of the finest melons to King Hung III with a message that they were a gift from his adopted son. Burdened with the tasks of running his kingdom, the king had forgotten all about An Tiem. The gift of melons jolted his memory and he ordered a boat to carry him to the island. He wanted to see for himself how An Tiem had fared.

When the king saw how An Tiem had built a successful life on a deserted island, he knew he had been wrong. He said, "My son, all you said about the seeds of the past determining the fruits of the future is clearly true. Your words were not those of an ungrateful son as I mistook them, but the words of one who believes in taking responsibility for his own actions."

The king asked An Tiem and his family to return to the mainland, and he gave An Tiem back his former post. Hao melons, or watermelons, were planted throughout the kingdom, and to this day, people recall the story of An Tiem when they taste the sweet red melon.

THE PINE GATE

IT WAS a chilly autumn evening, and the full moon had just risen, when the young swordsman arrived at the foot of the mountain. The wilderness was bathed in the light of the moon glimmering playfully on branches and leaves. It seemed that nothing had changed during the seven years he was away, and yet it was surprising that no one was there to greet him. The swordsman paused at the foot of the mountain and looked up. He saw that the narrow path up the mountain was barred by a tightly shut pine gate. He walked forward slowly and pushed at the gate, but it was immovable, even under his powerful hands.

Never, in as long as he could remember, had his master locked that gate. This narrow path was the only way up the mountain. So, holding onto the handle of his sword, he jumped as high as he could, but he was unable to jump over the low gate. A strange force had gripped his whole body and pushed it back down. Next, he unsheathed his long sword to cut the gate's bar open, but the sword's sharp blade bounced back from the soft pinewood with so power-ful an impact that it sent a shock through his hand and wrist. He raised his sword toward the sky and examined its edge under the moonlight. Somehow, the gate was too hard for his sword. It seemed that his master had endowed it with the strength of his own spirit. It was impassable. The swordsman sighed deeply, returned his sword to its sheath, and sat down on a rock outside the gate.

Seven years earlier, on the day he was to leave the mountain, his master looked into his eyes for a long moment without saying anything. There was a kind expression on his master's face, and yet there was something else too, perhaps a kind of pity. The young swordsman could only bow his head in reverence. After a while, the old man said to him, "I cannot keep you here forever. I know you have to go down the mountain and into the world to carry out the Way and help people. I thought I could keep you here with me a little longer, but if it is your will to leave now, you have all my blessings. Remember what I have taught you. In the world below, you will need it."

Then his master told him what to seek, what to avoid, and what to change. Finally, he put his gentle hand on his disciple's shoulder. "These are the main guidelines for your actions: Never do anything that might cause suffering to yourself or others, in the present or in the future. Go without fear in the direction that will lead yourself and others to complete awakening. And remember the standards by which happiness and suffering, liberation and illusion are measured. Without them, you betray the Way and will not help anyone.

"Here is my most precious sword. It is a sharp blade that comes from your own heart. Use it to subdue all evil and also to conquer all ambition and desire.

"Here is the *me ngo* glass," he said, handing his disciple a small viewing glass. "It will help you distinguish the wholesome from the unwholesome, the virtuous from the immoral. Sometimes it is called the Demon Viewer, for looking through it, you will be able to see the true forms of demons and evil spirits."

At daybreak the next morning, the young swordsman went up to the central hall to take leave of his master. The old man walked with him down the mountain, all the way to Tiger Brook, and there, amidst the murmuring of the mountain stream, master and disciple bade one another farewell. The master put his hand on the young man's shoulder, looked into his eyes, and said, "Remember, my child, poverty cannot weaken you, wealth cannot seduce you, power cannot vanquish you. I will be here the day you come back, your vows fulfilled!" The old man watched his disciple carefully as the young man took his leave and began the first steps of his journey.

While the first days of his journey remained vivid, the months and years that followed swirled through his mind. Humanity had revealed itself under so many different guises! How helpful the sword and the me ngo glass had been! Once, he met a monk, an old sage, whose appearance instantly inspired reverence. The old man invited him back to his hermitage to discuss how they might "join their efforts to help humankind." The young man listened with rapture, but then something struck him as odd about the old monk. He took out the me ngo glass and when he looked through it, he saw in front of him a giant demon with eyes sending forth crackling sparks, a horn on its forehead, and fangs as long as his own arms! The young man jumped back, drew his sword, and furiously attacked it. The demon fought back but, of course, it had no chance. It prostrated itself at the young man's feet, begging for mercy. The swordsman then demanded that it swear, under oath, to return to the place it had come from, study the Way, pray to be reborn as a human being, and refrain from ever disguising itself again as a monk to bewitch and devour the innocent.

Another time, he met a Mandarin, an old man with a long white beard. It was a happy encounter between a young hero out to save the world and a high official, a "father and mother to the people" bent on finding better ways to govern and benefit the masses. Again, the young man's suspicion was aroused, and under the glass, the handsome, awe-inspiring official turned out to be an enormous hog whose eyes literally dripped with greed. In an instant, the sword flew out of its sheath. The hog tried to flee, but the swordsman overtook it in one leap. Standing in front of the gate to the Mandarin's mansion, he barred the only escape route. The beast took on its true form and cried out loudly for mercy. Again, the young man did not leave without extracting from the monster the solemn oath that it would follow the Way and that it would never again take the form of a Mandarin to gnaw the flesh and suck the blood of the people.

Another time, walking by a marketplace, the young man saw a crowd surrounding a picture and book stall. The vendor was a beautiful young lady with a smile as radiant as a lotus opening to the sun. Seated nearby was another beautiful young lady singing softly while plucking the strings of a lute. The young ladies' beauty and the grace of the songs so captivated everyone present that no one left the stall once they had stopped. They could only stand and listen, enraptured, and buy pictures and books. Also drawn to the scene, the young man managed to make his way to the front, and he held up one of the pictures. The elegance of the design and strength of the colors overwhelmed him. Yet an uneasiness arose within him, and when he reached for his me ngo glass, he saw that the two beautiful girls were actually enormous snakes whose tongues darted back and forth like knife blades. The swordsman swept everyone aside in one movement of his arms, and with his sword pointing at the monsters, he shouted with a voice full of thunder, "Demons! Back to your evil nature!"

The crowd scattered in fright as the big snakes lashed at the young man. But as soon as his fabulous sword drew a few flashing circles around their bodies, the reptiles coiled at his feet in submission. He forced their jaws open, carved out their venomous fangs, and extracted the solemn promise that they would never come back to bewitch the village people. Then he burned down the bookstall and sent the monsters back to their lairs.

The young swordsman went from village to village and from town to town on his mission, offering people counsel and using his sword and his viewing glass to vanquish demons. He began to see himself as the "Indispensable Swordsman." He had come down from the mountain into a world where treachery and cunning reigned, and the world was surely better for his presence. He experienced great exhilaration in his actions for the good. At times, he even forgot to eat and sleep, the joy and satisfaction from helping people was so great.

Years passed quickly. One day, as he was resting alongside a river watching the water flow quietly by, he realized that he had not used the me ngo glass for some time. It was not that he had forgotten it. He just had not felt like using it. He remembered that at first he had used the glass reluctantly, and then had fought to the death every time he saw, through the me ngo, the true natures of the many evils that faced him. He recalled the great happiness he felt each time he saw, through the glass, the image of a virtuous man or a true sage.

Something had happened to him, and he didn't know what it was. He no longer felt much joy or fury whether he saw a sage or a monster. In fact, the monsters began to have a certain familiarity to him, even their horrifying features. The me ngo glass just remained safely in his pocket. The young swordsman thought about returning to the mountain someday to ask his master's advice. Why was he reluctant to use the me ngo glass, when it had clearly been of great help to him in the past?

On the twelfth day of the eighth month, seven years after he had left the mountain, he was walking through a forest of white plum trees, when suddenly, he yearned for the days when he studied under his old master, whose cottage also stood in an old plum forest.

Covered with snow-white plum blossoms under the autumn moon, he decided to return to the mountain.

He climbed many hills and crossed dozens of streams and, after seven days and seven nights, he reached the foot of the mountain. As he arrived, darkness was descending, and the rising moon revealed that the pine gate to the path up the mountain to his Master's abode was tightly shut. There was nothing he could do but wait. He could not go any further until one of his brothers came down to open the gate. At dawn, he thought, one of them will surely come down to fetch water from the stream, and they will open the gate for me. Now, the moon had risen and the entire mountain and forest were bathed in its cool light.

As the night wore on, the air became chillier. He pulled his sword out of the sheath and watched the moon's reflection on the sword's cold, sharp edge. Then he sheathed it again and stood up. The moon was extraordinarily bright. Mountain and forest were still, as if indifferent to the swordsman's presence. He dropped onto another rock, dejected, and the past seven years passed before him again. Slowly, the moon edged toward the summit of a distant mountain, and the stars shone brightly. Then they, too, began to recede, and there was a hint of glow in the east, as dawn was about to break.

The swordsman heard the rustling of dry leaves. He looked up and saw the vague form of someone walking down the mountains. It must be one of his younger brothers, he thought, though it was not light enough to be sure. The person was carrying something shaped like a large water jug. As the figure came closer and closer, the swordsman heard it exclaim, happily, "Elder Brother!"

"Younger Brother!"

"When did you arrive?"

"As the moon was just rising! I've been here all night. Why is the gate locked like this? Was it the master's order?"

The younger disciple raised his hand and pulled, ever so lightly, at the heavy gate. It swung open with ease. He stepped through it, and, grasping the swordsman's hands, looked at him and said, "You must be chilled to the bone. Look, you're covered with dew!

"My job used to be to come down here all day to pick herbs and watch the gate. If someone came who deserved an audience with the master, I'd bring him up. If I thought someone was not ready to see him, I'd just stay behind the bushes, and eventually they'd just give up! As you know, our master doesn't want to see anyone who does not have a true determination to learn.

"Lately, the master has allowed me to move on to more advanced studies, and as I stay up at the retreat most of the time, he told me to close the gate. He said it would open itself for anyone who is virtuous, but that it would bar the way for those too heavy with the dust of the world!"

The swordsman asked, "Would you say I am such a person? Why did the gate stay shut for me?"

The younger man laughed heartily, "Of course not! Anyway, we can go up now. But wait a moment, Elder Brother! I must first fetch some water. Will you come with me? Smile, Brother! Why are you so angry?"

Both men laughed. They made their way down to the stream. The sun was not yet up, but the east was already glowing brightly. The water was tinted a pale rose by the dawn, and the two men could see their reflections next to one another. The swordsman was bold and strong in his knight's suit, the long sword slung diagonally over his back. The younger disciple's figure was gentler in his flowing monk's robe, a jug in his hands. Without speaking, they looked at both reflections and smiled to one another. A water spider sprung up suddenly and caused the rose-tinted surface to ripple, sending their images into thousands of undulating patterns.

"How beautiful!" said the younger monk. "I would certainly destroy our reflections for good if I dipped the jug in now. By the way, do you still have the me ngo viewing glass with you? I remember that our master gave it to you when you came down the mountain years ago!"

The swordsman reached in his pocket to get it, and he realized that for all the years he was away, he had used the glass to look at others, but never once had he looked at himself through it. He took the glass out, wiped it on his sleeve, and aimed it at the water's surface. The two men's heads came close to look through the small glass together.

A loud scream escaped from the throats of both of them. It reverberated through the forest. The swordsman fell forward and collapsed. A deer, drinking water farther upstream, looked up in fright.

The younger disciple could not believe what he had seen. There he was in his flowing robe, jug in hand, standing next to a towering demon whose eyes were deep and dark like water wells and whose long fangs curved down around its square jaw. The demon's face was bluish gray, the shade of ashes and death. The young man shuddered and, rubbing his eyes, looked again at his senior, who was now lying unconscious on the blue stones of the riverbank, the older man's face still expressing shock and horror. Suffering had been etched upon his brother who, for seven years, had ceaselessly braved the rough and cruel world down below their mountain retreat.

The young disciple reached down to the stream to fetch water to douse his elder's face, and a moment later, the swordsman came to, his face ravaged with despair. His true image had appeared in the me ngo glass. Self-knowledge had come to him unexpectedly in such a swift, brutal fashion that he could do nothing but collapse under the blow. His energy had vanished. He tried to stand up, but he had no strength in his legs or arms.

"It's all right. It's all right, my elder brother! We'll go up now," the younger monk said.

To the swordsman's ears, his brother's voice was like a faint breeze murmuring from afar. He shook his head. His world had collapsed, and he no longer wanted to live. How could he bring himself into his beloved master's presence?

The younger man brushed the dirt off his brother's shoulder and spoke as if he had heard the swordsman's thoughts. "Don't worry. Our master has nothing but compassion for you. Let's go up now. We'll live and work and study together again."

The two figures made their way slowly up the steep, rock-strewn path that wound its way up the mountain. It was not yet day, and the silhouettes imprinted themselves on the thin veil of dew stretching over trees and rocks. The first rays of sun finally reached the two men. The shadow of the swordsman seemed only more broken in body and spirit next to the younger disciple whose steps were firm and whose mien was gentle.

Over the mountaintop, far away, the sun rose.

CONFLICT AND CHANGE

THE ANCIENT TREE

D EEP IN the forest highlands stood a great, ancient tree. No one knew how many thousands of years it had lived. Its trunk was as large as the arm spans of eighteen people. Its great roots pushed up through the ground and spread to a radius of fifty meters. Its bark was as hard as rock; if you pressed a fingernail against it, it would hurt your finger. Its branches held tens of thousands of birds' nests, sheltering hundreds of thousands of birds, large and small. The earth beneath the shadow of the tree was unusually cool.

In the morning when the sun rose, the first rays of light were like a conductor's baton beginning a grand symphony, the voices of the birds as majestic as any great philharmonic orchestra. All the creatures of the forest arose, on two feet or four, slowly and in awe.

In the great tree there was an opening as large as a grapefruit from Bien Hoa. It was twelve meters up from the ground. In that opening lay a small brown egg. No one could say if a bird had brought that egg there or if it had been formed by the sacred air of the forest and the life energy of the great tree.

Thirty years passed and the egg remained intact. During some nights, birds would be startled from their sleep by a brilliant light shining from the opening in the tree, illuminating an entire corner of the forest. Finally one night, under a very bright full moon and a brilliantly starlit sky, the egg cracked open and a tiny strange bird was born.

The bird gave a small chirp in the cold night; a cry neither tragic nor bold, but of surprise. She continued to cry throughout the night until the first rays of sunlight opened the morning symphony and thousands of birds' voices broke forth. From that moment on, the little bird cried no more.

The bird grew quickly. The nuts and grains that mother birds brought to the opening in the tree were always plenty. Soon the opening became too small, and the bird had to find a much larger home. She had taught herself to fly, and she gathered sticks and straw to build a new nest. Although the egg had been brown, the bird was as white as snow. Her wingspan was vast, and she always flew slowly and very quietly, often to faraway places where white waterfalls tumbled day and night like the majestic breath of earth and sky. Sometimes she did not return for several days. When she did return, she lay thoughtfully and quietly in her nest all day and night. Her two bright eyes never lost their look of surprise.

In the ancient Dai Lao Forest, a hermit's hut stood on the slope of a hill. There, a monk had lived for almost fifty years. The bird often flew across Dai Lao Forest, and from time to time she saw the monk walking slowly down the path to the spring holding a water jug in his hand. One day, the bird saw two monks walking together on the path leading from the spring to the hut. That night, concealed in the branches of a tree, the bird watched as the light of the fire flickered inside the hut and the two monks conversed the whole night long.

The bird flew high over the ancient forest, sometimes for days without landing. Below stood the great tree, and the creatures of mountain and forest hidden in the grass, bushes, and trees. From the day the bird overheard the exchange between the two monks, her curiosity grew. Where have I come from and where will I go? How many thousands of years will the great tree stand?

The bird had heard the two monks speak about time. What is time? Why has time brought us here, and why will it take us away? The nut that a bird eats has its own delicious nature. How can I find out the nature of time? The bird wanted to pick up a small piece of time and lie quietly with it in her nest to examine its nature. Even if it took months or years to examine, the bird was willing.

High over the ancient forest, the bird felt like a balloon drifting in nothingness. She felt her nature was as empty as a balloon's, and that emptiness was the base of her existence and the cause of her suffering as well. If I could find time, thought the bird, I could certainly find myself.

After many days and nights of flying and contemplating, the bird came quietly to rest in her nest. She had brought with her a tiny piece of earth from the Dai Lao Forest. Deep in thought, she picked up the piece of earth to examine it. The monk from the Dai Lao Forest had said to his friend, "Time is stilled in eternity, where love and your beloved are one.

"Each blade of grass, each piece of earth, each leaf, is one with that love."

But the bird was unable to find time. The clod of earth from Dai Lao Forest revealed nothing. Perhaps the monk had lied. Time lies in love, but where is love? The bird remembered the waterfalls endlessly tumbling in the Northwest Forest. She remembered the days she listened to the sounds of waterfalls from morn to eve. She even imagined herself tumbling like a waterfall, playing with the light sparkling on the water and caressing the pebbles and rocks down below. The bird felt like she herself was a waterfall, with endless water falling from her.

One noon, while flying across the Dai Lao Forest, the bird saw that the hut was no longer there. The whole forest had burned, and only a pile of ashes remained where the hut had been. In a panic, the bird flew around searching. The monk was no longer in the forest. Where had he gone? Corpses of animals. Corpses of birds. Had the fire consumed the monk? The bird was bewildered. Time, what are you? Why do you bring us here, and why will you take us away? The monk had said, "Time is stilled in eternity." If that is so, perhaps love has returned the monk to itself.

The bird flew swiftly back to the ancient forest, where anguished cries of many birds and explosions of bark revealed that the ancient forest was burning. Faster, faster still, the bird flew. The fire spread throughout the sky, and it spread near the great tree. Hundreds of thousands of birds shrieked in fright. As the fire approached the great tree, the bird flapped her wings feverishly, hoping to put it out, but the fire burned even more fiercely. The bird sped to the spring, dipped her wings in the water, and rushed back to shake the water over the forest. The drops just turned to steam. It was not enough, not enough. The bird's whole body soaked in water was not enough to extinguish the fire.

Hundreds of thousands of birds cried. Young birds without feathers to fly screamed. Then the fire began to burn the great tree. Why was there no rain? Why didn't the downpour that fell endlessly in the Northwest Forest flow like a waterfall here? The bird let forth a piercing cry, a cry both tragic and passionate, and suddenly the cry was transformed into the sound of a rushing waterfall. In that moment, the bird felt the fullness of her existence. Loneliness and emptiness vanished and the image of the monk, the image of the sun behind the mountain peak, and the image of the rushing water falling endlessly through a thousand lifetimes took their place. The cry of the bird had become the rush of the waterfall, and without fear the bird plunged into the forest fire like a majestic waterfall.

The next morning was calm. The rays of the sun shone, but there was no symphony, no sounds of thousands of birds. Parts of the forest had burned completely. The great tree stood, but more than half of its branches were charred. Corpses of large and small birds were everywhere. The forest was silent.

The birds that were still alive called one another, their voices betraying their bewilderment. By what grace had the clear sky suddenly poured forth rain, extinguishing the fire? They remembered seeing the great white bird shaking water from her two wings. They looked everywhere throughout the forest, but they could not find the white bird. Perhaps she had flown away to live in a different forest. Perhaps she had been killed by the fire. The great tree, its body charred and scarred with wounds, did not say a word. The birds turned their heads to the sky, and then began to build new nests in the remaining branches of the great tree. Did the ancient tree miss the child, the child of sacred mountain air and the life energy of its own four thousand years? Dear bird, where have you gone? Listen to the monk: time has returned the bird to the love that is the source of all things.

THE ONE NIGHT LAKE

EVERYONE in Ha Loa city knew the story of how the king's daughter, Tien Dung, came to marry Dong Tu, the son of a poor fisherman. As a child, Dong Tu lived with his widowed father near the small hamlet of Chu Xa. He was a good-natured boy and devoted son, dearly beloved by his father. Unfortunately, they were very poor and, even though they fished from early morning until dark, they earned barely enough to buy their rice.

One day while they swam in the river, their palm leaf hut caught fire. They returned home to find no more than a heap of ashes. Everything had been destroyed. Dong Tu had no clothing left, and all his father had was the ragged loincloth he was already wearing. There was nothing to do but gather branches and build a new hut. Because they owned only one article of clothing between them, they could no longer go to market together to sell their fish. One was always obliged to stay at home.

Not long after that, Dong Tu's father fell deathly ill. He summoned Dong Tu to his bedside and said, "When I die, do not bury me in the loincloth. Please keep it for yourself. I do not want anyone to laugh at you because you have no clothes." He then closed his eyes and left this world.

Dong Tu loved his father too much to bury him without the loin-cloth. Because Dong Tu now had nothing to wear, he could no longer go to market. Instead he stood waist deep in the river and sold fish to passing boats.

One day as he sat on the riverbank digging bait worms, he noticed some elegant boats in the distance. The sound of drums and singing drifted on the air from the boats, which he could tell bore the royal family's emblem. Suddenly he realized that the boats were headed towards shore. Before long they would moor close to where he sat. Afraid to be discovered without any clothes on, Dong Tu frantically dug a hole in the sand and buried himself, leaving a small breathing hole. When the boats docked, Princess Tien Dung, the daughter of King Hung Vuong IV, stepped onto shore with her attendants. It was her custom to take a boat trip every spring to visit distant regions of her father's kingdom.

After a brief stroll, she asked her attendants to set up a screen behind which she could bathe in private. Unknown to her ladies-in-waiting, they placed the screen close to where Dong Tu had con-cealed himself. Princess Tien Dung began to bathe. As she splashed water over herself, it washed away the sand covering Dong Tu. Ter-rified, Dong Tu flipped over like a fish. While startled to discover the presence of this stranger, Tien Dung kept calm. She said, "Please use the rest of the water in my bucket to rinse the sand off yourself. Wait here and I will bring you some clothes."

She quickly dressed and gave her attendants strict orders not to remove the screen. She found a set of men's clothing on her boat and brought it back for Dong Tu. When she emerged again from behind the screen accompanied by a strange young man, her attendants stared in astonishment. Nonplussed, the princess invited Dong Tu to join her for tea and lunch aboard her boat. She asked Dong Tu to tell her about himself.

When Tien Dung learned how Dong Tu had buried his father in their only remaining article of clothing, she gazed at him with deep admiration. She said, "An intelligent and good-hearted person like you should not have to live in such misery. I believe the unusual circumstances surrounding our meeting today are due to some connection we share from a past life. For some time, my father has wanted me to marry, but I have always refused. Now that I have met you, I feel we were meant to be together. If you agree, we could marry."

Dong Tu tried hard to refuse her offer, not because he feared the princess held too elevated a position, but because he thought he must be dreaming. At last he gave in to Tien Dung's persuasion. He had never considered marriage before, but he felt a natural kinship with this young princess whose name, which meant "Beauty of a Goddess," fit her well.

The princess was not naive. She knew that if she explained to her father how she and Dong Tu met, he would never grant permission for their marriage. But Tien Dung had little patience with the restrictions of royal life. She announced they would celebrate their marriage at once in Chu Xa hamlet. After the ceremony, she sent her attendants back to the capital to inform the king and to make a formal request that he accept their marriage.

King Hung was enraged when he learned that his daughter had married a commoner she met on her travels without even seeking permission from her parents. He shouted, "Let her do what she likes! From this moment, I will have nothing more to do with her!" Though he loved his headstrong daughter, she had embarrassed him before his court and he knew of no way to defend her shocking behavior.

Far away, Tien Dung and Dong Tu sailed into the harbor of Ha Loa. Liking the scenery, they decided to settle there. They sold the boat and Tien Dung's belongings in order to build a house and set up a small business. They purchased sandalwood and spices from local people to trade with the occasional foreign traders who set anchor in Ha Loa. During spells of stormy weather when the traders were stranded, Tien Dung and Dong Tu offered them lodging in their own home. Dong Tu proved adept at learning foreign languages from their guests.

Before long, they were running a successful business. Others, assisted by Tien Dung, also set up trade in Ha Loa. She was especially devoted to helping poor families get on their feet. Foreign traders stopped ever more frequently and stayed longer in Ha Loa, until the sleepy town grew into a bustling center of trade. Because Tien Dung and Dong Tu were both gracious and honest, foreign

traders were always eager to do business with them. Dong Tu's ability to speak their languages further enhanced the business. Natives
of Ha Loa loved the enterprising couple, as well. Tien Dung never
acted like a spoiled princess who expected special privileges. She was
warm and kind-hearted to all she met, and devoted herself to efforts
to help the less fortunate. Although Ha Loa was soon a good-sized
city, there was not a single soldier or policeman in sight. Following
Tien Dung and Dong Tu's example of virtue and generosity, the people lived in peace and harmony.

One spring, an Indian trader stayed with the couple for more than
a month. When he prepared to return home, he invited Dong Tu to
accompany him. He said, "Bring just one bar of gold and I will help
you buy fine silks and other precious items that you can sell for a
great profit. Plan on staying for several weeks and I will introduce
you to my country. I would be most grateful if you would allow me
this chance to repay all your kindness."

At first Dong Tu hesitated, but Tien Dung encouraged him. "My
good husband, please accept this invitation. I can manage our affairs
in your absence. Don't pass up this opportunity. Think of all the new
people you will meet and all the wonderful things you will learn."

And so Dong Tu agreed to go. After sailing a month, the ship
anchored at a port where mountains met the sea, in order to replenish food and water supplies. Dong Tu went ashore with some of the
sailors and gazed up at the lofty peaks. The sailors pointed out a
tiny hut high up on one of the slopes which they said belonged to
a hermit named Buddhabhadra who practiced the Way.

One sailor said, "We'll be anchored here for at least half a day.
Why don't you stretch your legs and go up to see the hermit yourself?"

Curious, Dong Tu nodded and began the long ascent. When he
reached the hut, there was no one in sight. But when he walked to

the back of the hut, he found a man meditating on a large stone beneath a tree. The monk's face radiated such peace and calm that Dong Tu felt refreshed just looking at him. The monk opened his eyes and smiled at Dong Tu. He said, "I have been waiting for you. What has taken you so long?"

Dong Tu was surprised. "What do you mean?"

The hermit replied, "Because of links in a past life, you and I were destined to meet in this life. It is my duty to show you the Way."

"The way to where?" asked the puzzled Dong Tu.

"The way to inner peace," replied the monk. "The fortunes of this world constantly rise and fall, but the heart of one who has attained the Way is never without peace and freedom. You possess all that is needed to realize the Way. Stop seeking wealth and seek the treasures of your mind instead."

Buddhabhadra's words lifted a weight from Dong Tu's heart. He sat down to listen to more of the monk's teaching, which refreshed him like gentle rain on the parched earth.

When it was time to set sail again, one of the sailors came to fetch Dong Tu, but Dong Tu said, "Kindly inform my friend to sail on without me. I have decided to remain here to study the Way. When my friend makes the return trip, please ask him to fetch me on the way back to Ha Loa."

Dong Tu's friend climbed the mountain to try to persuade him to continue the journey, but Dong Tu would not be swayed. Dong Tu said, "Dear friend, you can take my bar of gold and buy the merchandise for me. I now have a rare opportunity that presents itself only once in a thousand years. Please understand."

His friend did not press him further. He bid Dong Tu farewell and promised to retrieve Dong Tu on the return journey. He wanted to leave them food supplies but the monk refused, saying, "There is plenty of fruit growing wild here for us to eat."

Four months passed. For the first time, Dong Tu tasted the joys of meditation. He discovered how to release sorrow and anxiety and to find ease for his mind and body. He saw there was no need to chase after anything in this life.

When the ship returned, Dong Tu's friend was surprised to find him sitting serenely in meditation. Dong Tu was reluctant to leave but Buddhabhadra told him, "You have not completed your predestined relationship to the kingdom of Van Lang. It is time for you to return." The hermit gave Dong Tu a walking stick, a straw hat, and a begging bowl. He said, "Guard these three things. One who follows the Way needs nothing more. These three things can produce miracles."

Dong Tu bowed reverently to his teacher and accepted the gifts.

Two months later, the ship arrived in Ha Loa. Tien Dung found her husband somehow changed. He seemed removed from their busy world. As he began to recount his months with Buddhabhadra, Tien Dung was filled with a strange happiness. She asked Dong Tu to share the monk's teaching with her. Dong Tu recited sutras he had learned and showed his wife how to observe her breathing in order to meditate. He showed her how she could master her thoughts and develop her powers of concentration.

Once Tien Dung tasted the joys of meditation, she proposed they give all their belongings away. They sold their houses, shops, and merchandise and gave the money to poor families to enable them to buy farms and businesses of their own. Dong Tu and Tien Dung kept only the stick, hat, and begging bowl. Though people invited them to sleep in their homes, they refused, preferring to sleep beneath the trees. The straw hat sheltered them from sun and rain, and they used the stick to clear paths in the forest. Whenever they received an offering of food in their bowl, they recited sutras and taught the people about the Way. They lived a life of peace, devoted to meditation, and were unburdened by any cares or fears.

Back in the capital city of Phong Chau, King Hung knew nothing of these things. But he had received several disturbing reports
about the number of foreigners living in the prospering city of Ha
Loa. Some of his advisors claimed that the princess and her husband
were plotting to overthrow the throne and they urged the king to
send soldiers to quell rebellion in Ha Loa.

Not long after that, news reached Ha Loa that a battalion of government troops were on their way to raze the city. The army was
less than a day's march away. In terrible panic, the people prepared
to flee Ha Loa. Throughout the city, everyone swarmed like frantic
bees. City elders came looking for Tien Dung and Dong Tu in hopes
they might offer some solution to the crisis.

Tien Dung and Dong Tu received the news calmly. They knew it
was impossible for all of Ha Loa to be evacuated safely in one day.
Those left behind would be helpless against the attack by government soldiers who would, no doubt, be expecting armed resistance.
After speaking with the city elders, Dong Tu sat silently in meditation beneath a cork tree. He hoped to find a solution that would
prevent needless bloodshed and untold suffering. The elders conversed quietly with Tien Dung as they waited for the fruits of Dong
Tu's meditation.

Dong Tu opened his eyes and smiled. He had found a way to help
the people. He stretched his legs and then turned to the elders. "I
know a way to delay the soldiers' arrival for three days and nights.
That will provide you with enough time to evacuate the people safely.
Please ask the people to remain calm and tell them that any danger
can be overcome if they remember to take care of each other."

The elders returned to the city. They had complete confidence in
Dong Tu.

Carrying the hat, stick, and bowl, Dong Tu and Tien Dung walked
down to the river. There they borrowed a small boat to cross to the

other shore. The princess was curious to hear what Dong Tu's plan was. She looked at him and he said, "There is a passage in the Lotus Sutra in which a city suddenly appears in the desert. Accustomed to a simple life, you and I have no need of a city or a palace. A tree is enough shelter for us. A tree, a hat, or a stick—it's all the same." Though she did not yet fully grasp her husband's meaning, Tien Dung nodded.

It was dusk when they reached the other shore. They secured the boat to a tree, and followed a path between fields of rice until they reached a high hill. Dong Tu placed the stick in the ground at the top of the hill. He set the hat on it and the bowl beside it. Tien Dung joined him in sitting meditation.

Then the miracle took place. A huge palace appeared where the hill had been. It was surrounded by hundreds of dwellings and shops. A prosperous city spread before them protected by high walls and a moat. There were sounds of people and animals rushing back and forth from within the walls.

Off in the distance, government soldiers caught their first glimpse of flickering lights from the great city. Because they were weary after their long march, the generals ordered the troops to set up camp and rest several hours.

At midnight, the soldiers received orders to attack. In a flash, they had the city surrounded. The city gates were tightly barricaded and could not be opened. Despite all their efforts the soldiers were unable to penetrate the thick walls. There was nothing to do but lay siege and wait until the people surrendered. Three days passed. No one entered or exited the city.

On the third night, a night of many stars but no moon, one of the government sentries gazed at a particularly bright star and suddenly heard a strange voice whisper in his ear, "Three days and nights have passed. Everyone has safely evacuated the city."

Startled, he turned towards the besieged city. All was silent. He looked into the sky for the bright star only to discover that black clouds covered the skies. A violent wind appeared from nowhere. A vicious storm broke. Trees were uprooted and tents sent flying. Without warning, a tornado swept the entire city from sight. Panic-stricken soldiers scrambled for cover. It looked like the aftermath of a terrible defeat.

Before long, the wind died down and all was calm again. As the first light of dawn appeared over the horizon, the soldiers saw that there was an immense lake where the city used to be.

Later that same day, other army scouts arrived to inform the generals that the real city of Ha Loa was completely deserted. Houses and gardens were empty. There was not so much as a cow, buffalo, duck, or chicken. The generals did not know what to make of the strange situation.

In just one night an entire city had disappeared, leaving a lake in its place. Efforts to locate Princess Tien Dung and Dong Tu were fruitless. Before returning to the capital, one general stood staring at the lake and whispered, "A one night lake. . ."

Ha Loa was not attacked again. The people returned and once again the city prospered. Many of Ha Loa's inhabitants continued to practice the Way and to teach it to others. Tien Dung and Dong Tu were not seen again in those parts. Perhaps, the people mused, they had traveled to a distant mountain to follow the Way in peace. But whenever the people looked at One Night Lake, they recalled the beautiful princess and her good-hearted husband who had been so kind to them.

The Magic Warrior

King Hung Vuong waited anxiously for news. Invading troops were closing in on the northern border of his kingdom Van Lang. Although he had prepared three years for this invasion, he still waited for the special sign promised by Dragon Emperor. He remembered how three years ago he met with his advisors to discuss the growing threat posed by the neighboring country of An.

One advisor had counseled, "If they send troops, we will be forced to fight. Thus far, however, they have made only verbal threats. Rather than make full-scale preparations for war, let us first train a special corps of generals and soldiers ready to mobilize in case of an attack."

Another advisor said, "The king of An is a fierce warrior. If he decides to invade, I fear for our kingdom. Our people have lived in peace for centuries and do not know the ways of war. The soldiers of An possess many kinds of deadly weapons. Your Highness, we must turn to Dragon Emperor for assistance."

The king had a special altar built that was thirty feet long. He made incense offerings and for three days and nights fasted and slept on the ground by the altar. Then he began to pray, invoking the name of Dragon Emperor.

Black clouds gathered in the sky. There was a crash of thunder after which a guard came running to inform the king that an old man, standing more than fifteen feet tall, was outside requesting an audience with the king. He had a long white beard and bushy eyebrows. The king himself went outside to welcome the old man. The man, who had been singing and dancing while waiting for the guard's return, grew suddenly silent. When the king offered him tea, he made no gesture to accept it.

King Hung addressed the silent stranger, "Most respected Sir, the king of An is planning to invade Van Lang. We do not know how our kingdom will fare. Please allow us to ask your counsel in this matter."

The old man gazed a long moment at his hand and then said, "An troops will not invade for another three years."

"How can we best prepare to defend ourselves?"

The old man answered, "Train a special force of skilled warriors. No doubt you have already thought of that. When the first An troops are spotted along the border, seek a general from among the people who can lead you to sudden victory. I cannot reveal beforehand who that person will be. Do not discriminate against the one who promises victory, regardless of whether he is rich or poor, young or old. River God will assist me in this matter."

Having spoken, the old man floated up into the air and disappeared among the clouds. The king understood then that he had been speaking to Dragon Emperor himself.

Three years passed. The first troops had been spotted. The special force of warriors was dispatched to the border. At the same time, delegates were sent throughout the country to seek the general who could promise sudden victory. Days passed with no word.

Then one day, one of the delegates returned saying he had an urgent message. The king and his advisors listened to all he had to say.

"Your Majesty, people throughout the kingdom have expressed their utmost faith in your ability to repel the invaders. When we said we were seeking a general from among the people, everyone claimed they were ignorant of military affairs and placed their trust in your warriors. Discouraged, we continued our search. Then a strange thing happened in the tiny village of Phu Dong. When we read your decree,

a

young woman approached us and insisted we follow her back to her home. When we entered her hut, we didn't see anyone but a toddler playing alone on the bed. He looked straight at us and said, 'Honorable Sirs, what message do you bear from the king?'

"At first we didn't want to waste time talking to a child, but the woman prevented us from leaving and said, 'Three years ago, I gave birth to the child you see here. For three years, he did nothing but lie in his bed. He never sat up and he never made a sound, not even *Mama* or *Papa*. But today when he heard us talking about the arrival of the king's delegates, he sat right up and said, "Mother, go and invite the king's delegates to come speak with me." It seemed a miracle, and so I wasted no time in bringing you here. What do you suppose it means?'"

The delegate continued, "We turned to listen to the child and this is what he told us, 'Please, Sirs, return at once to the capital. Ask the king to make an iron horse that is fifteen feet high, an iron sword ten feet long, and an iron helmet fit for a giant. I will need those three things to turn back the invaders. Bring them to me as soon as possible and remember, they must be made of iron, not copper.'"

One of the king's advisors burst out laughing, "How preposterous! Your messengers are wasting your precious time with children's fancies!"

But King Hung did not laugh. Instead he asked, "Gentlemen, do you know what iron is? The child said the horse, sword, and helmet must be made of iron, not copper."

Another advisor said, "Your Majesty, I know what iron is. It is a very special kind of metal that is unusually hard. Copper is solid but nothing compared to iron. Last year a foreign trader who is a friend of mine sent me a small iron knife as a gift. If you will allow it, I will go fetch it at once."

When the advisor returned, he pulled the knife from its sheath. A chill ran down the spines of the other advisors when they saw how smooth and shiny the knife was. The king took the knife and struck a copper urn with it. A large dent was left in the urn. The king examined the knife. There was not even a scratch upon it.

The king said, "This iron is indeed a special metal. If we could acquire it, we could make weapons stronger than any known before. But where can we find more of this iron?"

Just at that moment, a guard entered to announce that a messenger from the River God desired an audience with the king. This man, too, was old with a long white beard and bushy eyebrows. When he was ushered in, he did not wait to be addressed before speaking. "Your Majesty, I can help you procure the iron you and your generals seek. This stone rod which serves as my staff will lead you to places where iron is buried deep in the earth. Wave it over the ground. You will feel a tug when you are over the right places. There you must dig until you find the iron. The iron you unearth will be mixed with other elements that you must separate out by heating the iron in a blazing furnace. Once it has been purified, you will be able to make tools and weapons."

The old man handed the walking stick to the king, who respectfully accepted it. He invited the man to stay for a banquet in his honor, but the old man declined, so the king asked his guard to accompany the man out of the palace. When they reached the river shore, the old man turned into a huge golden turtle and disappeared beneath the water.

Thanks to the stone rod, iron was found. Workers dug day and night and then heated the metal to filter out impurities. It took two months to manufacture the horse, sword, and helmet requested by the child. When they were completed, the king arranged for them to be transported by river barge to Phu Dong village. Then the king ordered his workers to refine and mold more of the iron into swords, 30,000 in all, for his soldiers.

In Phu Dong village, the child turned to his mother and said, "The king's barge will soon be here. Please cook me a pot of rice. I must prepare for battle."

His mother cooked a large pot of rice and was astonished when he ate it all and asked for more. Over the next few days, he ate as much as one hundred men. All the families in the village were kept busy bringing him rice, vegetables, and cakes. His appetite seemed endless, but no one resented bringing him food, for they knew he was a special envoy from Dragon Emperor who would save their country. Neighboring villages contributed food, as well, and cloth to sew him clothes. A pair of pants lasted him no more than one or two days before he outgrew them.

The same day the barge arrived in Phu Dong, the king received news that invading troops from An had crossed the border and defeated the king's special forces. The invaders were flooding into Van Lang as the people scattered in terror.

It was after sunset before the iron horse, sword, and helmet were unloaded from the barge. The delegates made their way to the child's hut and discovered it surrounded by great sacks of rice. The child asked his mother and the villagers to prepare a feast to share with the king's delegates. Even after everyone had eaten their fill, the child continued eating. He ate all night long. Only when the first cock crowed did he put down his bowl.

With a great stretch, he stood up. He was more than twenty feet tall. He put on his helmet and grabbed his iron sword. He jumped onto the iron horse and exclaimed in a voice as deep as thunder, "I am the Magic Warrior sent by Goddess Au Co and Dragon Emperor to save our people!" The iron horse stirred as if alive. Sparks of fire flew from its flaring nostrils, and it reared back and pierced the skies with a cry. The Magic Warrior galloped off to meet the advancing An troops.

When the Magic Warrior reached the foot of Trau Son Mountain, he found soldiers of both sides engaged in heavy combat. Van Lang soldiers were holding their own, armed with shining new swords of iron. The Magic Warrior, his sword flashing, galloped straight into the ranks of the invaders. Many dropped dead, including the king of An. Others were surrounded and forced to surrender.

The Magic Warrior chased fleeing An troops past Viet Soc Mountain until he was certain they would not return. Then he turned and galloped straight up the mountain. He and the iron horse were never seen again, though traces of the horse's mighty hoofprints can still be seen all the way up the mountain.

King Hung rejoiced at the news of victory. He only regretted he had not been able to meet the Magic Warrior in person. He ordered an altar to be built at the foot of Viet Soc Mountain so that the people of Van Lang would never forget the Magic Warrior of Phu Dong.

The king knew that a twenty-foot-tall warrior who rode a fire-spitting iron horse could not remain on Earth among ordinary mortals. But though the Magic Warrior returned to his place among the gods, the soldiers of Van Lang had something to remember him by. Their iron weapons would help them protect the kingdom from future invasions. In that way the Magic Warrior was still among them.

PRINCESS SITA

T HE IMMORTALS Son Vuong and Thuy Vuong were brothers. Thuy Vuong lived in the sea and Son Vuong lived in the mountains. Once Thuy Vuong came to visit his brother in the mountains and stayed several months. Before he returned, he invited Son Vuong to visit the sea, and Son Vuong accepted.

Because Son Vuong was so kind-hearted, he was loved by all the sea creatures he met. Thuy Vuong, on the other hand, was stubborn and hotheaded, with many sea monsters at his command. Dragon Emperor, burdened with other tasks, had appointed Thuy Vuong rain-bearer from July to December. Princess Sita, Dragon Emperor's beloved daughter, was in charge of the rains that fell from January through June.

After several months, Son Vuong grew weary of the agitated life beneath the sea and longed for the serenity of the high mountains. So he returned to land and, with a calm and relaxed heart, rowed a small boat along the rivers of Van Lang until he reached the majestic peaks of Tam Dao. He chose to live on the highest peak, Tan Vien, which was shaped like a perfect parasol and pierced the white clouds.

Son Vuong took many long walks over neighboring mountains,

dabbled in clear springs, climbed trees, and enjoyed the breathtak-
ing view from his own mountain. Sometimes he sat along the Chiet
Giang River and watched the fish swim by, reminiscing about his
time spent beneath the sea. He found the people in the villages below
to be kind and honest, and he enjoyed visiting them. He showed the
local people ways to irrigate their rice fields. He helped them fashion wooden and copper plows and introduced cotton as a crop. He
showed the people how they could spin thread and weave cloth.
The people did not dye their cloth brown or green like the people
of other regions, and so they were known as the white-clothed mountain people.

Before Son Vuong's arrival, the people made homes from rough-
hewn logs and covered their walls with sheaves of long grasses. Son
Vuong showed them how to build huts on stilts. He taught them
how to split bamboo to make sturdy walls and how to weave grasses
into rain-tight roofs. Little by little, the people's lives improved thanks
to Son Vuong, and they affectionately called him King of Tan Vien
Mountain.

One time Son Vuong returned to the sea palace to enlist Dragon
Emperor's aid in destroying a fox spirit that ate human flesh. It was
a thousand-year-old fox spirit that lived in a cave at the foot of Tien
Thach Mountain, and it often changed shape. Sometimes it appeared
as a monkey, sometimes as a human being. In human form, it was
perfectly disguised in white cotton clothes. It mingled with the village girls and boys, joining their songs and dances. Sometimes it lured
several children to its cave, where it ate them. Because it could change
shape at will and had many hidden entrances and exits to its cave,
it was impossible to catch.

Dragon Emperor caused water to rise, flooding the entrance to
every cave on Tien Thach Mountain. The fox spirit was forced to
emerge, and Son Vuong destroyed it as it fled up the mountain. The

people were able to live once more without fear, and Son Vuong could again enjoy the beauty of his mountain home, undisturbed.

On another day as he sat by the Chiet River, Son Vuong suddenly noticed a tiny pink fish waving her tail at him. He cupped his hands and gently scooped the fish out of the water, and she transformed herself into a young woman.

"Sita!" exclaimed Son Vuong.

Dragon Emperor's beloved daughter had turned into a little fish to play in the mountain brooks. She sat by Son Vuong and asked him about his life in the mountains. He invited her to visit his home on Tan Vien peak. Along the way, they passed several hamlets. Sita was charmed by the white-clothed people, who regarded her with both curiosity and affection. Seeing how Son Vuong and the people placed their palms together like a lotus bud to greet each other, Sita did the same.

It was noon when they reached Son Vuong's lofty, solitary home. Sita admired the view below—tiny huts clustered near thickets of lush bamboo and rivers winding through cotton fields, orchards, and rice paddies. Wisps of white cloud drifted overhead, while other clouds concealed the mountain's peak. Mountain goats approached them, and Son Vuong fed them fresh leaves. Birds came to rest on Sita's hands, twittering gaily. Son Vuong gave her grains of rice to offer them.

Sita turned to Son Vuong and said, "Son, it is truly wonderful here. So peaceful. But I feel you lack one thing."

"What is that?"

"The presence of a woman."

Son Vuong laughed, "But you're here right now! Why don't you visit more often? I would be glad to come meet you by the Chiet River."

Sita smiled. "I do not mean just any woman. There is only one

woman worthy to live here with you." She paused, and then added
teasingly, "But I can't tell you who she is."

Son Vuong returned her smile. "Very well, do not tell me."

Sita stayed until evening. Son Vuong accompanied her back down
the mountain. They stopped by a brook where Sita said, "This will
do. I can follow this brook to the river and from there return to the
sea."

She looked into Son Vuong's eyes and said, "That woman I mentioned lives in Phong Chau. No other woman can match her beauty.
She is a princess, the only daughter of King Hung Vuong XVIII. She
is called Mi Nuong. Go early tomorrow to Phong Chau and ask for
her hand."

Holding onto a pine branch, Sita stepped into the gurgling brook.
She bent over and turned back into a tiny pink fish that waved its
tail good-bye, and then disappeared.

Son Vuong climbed back up the mountain. The goats were graz-
ing peacefully and the birds came to sit on his shoulders. He entered
his cave and took out a jug of wine and a small cup. As he drank,
he quietly gazed about. His eyes came to rest on the chessboard he
had carved on a flat rock. Suddenly his home seemed empty. Perhaps the sea princess was right. He would follow her advice and go
to Phong Chau in the morning. He wanted at least to meet the beautiful Mi Nuong.

When Son Vuong arrived at the king's palace in the morning, he
discovered Thuy Vuong was also there. He greeted his brother but
did not ask what business brought him to Phong Chau. He did not
need to, for Thuy Vuong said, "Yesterday evening, I happened to
meet Sita. I asked her where she had been and she told me. I wanted
to know the purpose of her visit but she refused to speak. Only
when I grabbed her by the throat did she confess. So, you're coming to seek the hand of Mi Nuong, are you? Well, I've had the same

idea for a long time now and I intend to marry her. We'll see who wins this one."

Son Vuong smiled uneasily but said nothing. A palace guard invited them both in for an audience with the king. King Hung invited them to sit on a jewel-encrusted couch. He stroked his long white beard and asked, "By what good fortune do I have the privilege of receiving two immortals today?"

Thuy Vuong spoke first, "I have come to ask Your Majesty for Mi Nuong's hand. I am prepared to satisfy any of your conditions."

King Hung turned towards Son Vuong, "And please, what is your purpose in coming here today?"

Son Vuong spoke in a calm, respectful voice, "Your Majesty, I have come, as well, to ask for the princess in marriage."

King Hung stroked his beard and chuckled somewhat nervously. "Alas that I have but one daughter. Otherwise, this could all be arranged quite easily."

An advisor sitting beside the king made a suggestion. "Your Majesty, our country is threatened with betrayal by the Thuc clan. Although they occupy only a small area at present, they are gaining strength. Select the immortal who possesses the greatest power to protect our kingdom."

"That is a good idea," agreed the king, "but how do we test their powers?"

Before anything more could be said, Thuy Vuong raised his hand in a special gesture and chanted a complicated mantra. Suddenly, the clear sky turned black with clouds. Thunder exploded and the deafening roars of sea monsters filled the air. Then Thuy Vuong made another gesture, and all was quiet again. The sky became clear and sunny. Everyone turned towards the mountain god. Leaning only slightly forward, Son Vuong swept his hand across the courtyard. To everyone's amazement his hand turned into a hill on which they were all sitting. The hill rose higher and higher until it was a mountain touching the clouds. The city of Phong Chau was no more than a speck below. Then the mountain steadily lowered back down. Son Vuong removed his hand and they found themselves again sitting in the same places in the palace courtyard. Son Vuong's serene expression had not changed but the color was drained from Thuy Vuong's face.

The king declared, "Clearly, you both possess formidable powers. It would be impossible to judge the stronger of the two. Perhaps I should ask Mi Nuong her own feelings. After all, this affair concerns her most directly, does it not?"

A young woman entered the courtyard. She was as beautiful as early spring. She had willowlike tresses, a forehead like the rising dawn, and lips like a lotus. Her walk was as graceful as rice plants swaying in a tender breeze. Son Vuong was filled with wonder and respect. Princess Sita was right. There could be no woman more beautiful than Mi Nuong. Thuy Vuong eyed her with feverish desire. He was not about to let her fall into the hands of his brother.

Mi Nuong spoke in a voice as gentle as raindrops on a lotus pond. "My Father, please command that the god who arrives first tomorrow morning with the wedding offerings shall be my groom."

The king nodded. He addressed the two gods, "So be it. Tomorrow, I will offer Mi Nuong to the god who arrives first. Remember, your gifts should be worthy of a royal wedding."

The two gods bowed and departed.

In the early mists of dawn, Son Vuong arrived. All night long, the white-clothed mountain people, the deer, and the birds had helped him gather gifts worthy of a royal wedding. His massive carriage pulled by twenty mountain deer was laden with sandalwood, cinnamon, and many other treasures. He pulled on the reins and led the carriage into the palace courtyard.

King Hung and Mi Nuong were both awake and waiting. Mi Nuong clutched her father's hand and tears filled her eyes as she bid him farewell. He walked with her to the kneeling Son Vuong. The king bid him rise and said, "I am happy you are the first to arrive. I feel certain my daughter is, too. Receive now the most precious jewel in all the kingdom. We depend on you to protect the throne."

Son Vuong began to prostrate in gratitude, but the king urged him to depart before his brother arrived. As Son Vuong and his bride departed in their carriage, two teardrops fell from the king's eyes. He wiped them with his sleeve and then turned to enter the palace.

As they drove off, Mi Nuong said, "I knew you would be the first to arrive and that is why I set the condition I did."

Son Vuong did not speak, but instead he leaned over and tenderly kissed Mi Nuong's hair. He pulled at the reins to encourage his deer to make speed.

It was noon before Thuy Vuong arrived at the palace. He was accompanied by dozens of servants bearing trays piled with pearls, coral, and other treasures. He asked the palace guards to announce his arrival. When there was no response from the king, he grew impatient but tried to keep his composure. Only after having his arrival announced several times with no acknowledgment by the king did he grab the arm of a nearby guard and snarl, "Has the mountain god already been here?"

The guard cried out in pain and begged the sea god to release his arm. "Son Vuong came at the break of dawn. True to his word, the king gave Mi Nuong's hand to the suitor who arrived first. Son Vuong has taken the princess to his mountain home."

Thuy Vuong screamed in rage. His cries shook the entire palace. The king hurried out and tried to console the disappointed suitor, but Thuy Vuong scattered the trays of refreshments that were offered with a shove of his mighty arm. He ran from the palace while reciting a mantra. Immediately black clouds appeared from nowhere, thunder crashed, and rain began to fall in endless torrents, flooding every river and overflowing into houses and fields. Seawater began to rise until it engulfed the foot of Tan Vien Mountain, while sea monsters under Thuy Vuong's command invaded from all directions. Thuy Vuong was determined to force Son Vuong to hand over the princess.

Son Vuong and Mi Nuong were high up the mountain, safe from Thuy Vuong's attacks, but when they witnessed the tragic plight of the people below, they organized rescue efforts. Son Vuong mobilized deer and goats to haul the people's belongings up the mountain to safety. He spread a vast net around the foot of the mountain to trap sea monsters. He showed the people how to press on crocodiles' necks with long sticks while others bound their feet and jaws with strong rope. Mi Nuong hastily led mothers and their children to safety, while Son Vuong hurled boulders down on the heads of sea monsters.

Thuy Vuong could see that defeating Son Vuong would be no easy feat. Whenever he raised the level of the water, Son Vuong caused the land to rise. Tan Vien Mountain soared ever higher, surpassing even the clouds. Corpses of sea monsters killed by boulders floated on the waves. Frantic, Thuy Vuong transformed himself into a ruthless sea monster, thousands of feet long, called Makara. Its thrashing limbs created mammoth waves that slapped against the mountain. Even worse, it spat a black venom that scorched the flesh of humans and sea creatures alike. The ghastly cries of poisoned victims shook the skies. Son Vuong was filled with anguish. He urged Mi Nuong to lead the people even higher, beyond the reach of the black waters, as he hurled boulders down on the head of Makara.

In the midst of the fighting, Princess Sita appeared as a rainbow-colored fish. She saw the suffering borne by both sides. Her tears turned into drops of jade as she swam among the wounded. With a sudden twist of her body, she turned into an enormous dragon which swallowed all the water polluted by Makara's black venom. Though it burned her throat and stomach, she did not stop until she had swallowed it all. She dragged her great body onto shore to create a canal that provided a way to drain the floodwaters and block the passage of sea monsters. Thuy Vuong was enraged but there was nothing more he could do. He ordered his forces to withdraw, vowing that he would be back to seize Mi Nuong no matter what the cost.

Son Vuong and Mi Nuong descended the mountain the next morning to survey the destruction. Homes had been washed away. People burned by Makara's poison writhed on the ground. The bodies of drowned cattle, chickens, and ducks were strewn everywhere. The rice fields were ruined. Palm and bamboo trees were left in shreds. The survivors were doing their best to clear the wreckage and begin the process of rebuilding. No one spoke a word of blame against Son Vuong or Mi Nuong, but they shook their heads, lamenting so great a loss of life. Never before had brothers fought so fiercely.

That evening, Son Vuong and Mi Nuong heard a moan as they passed by a cave at the foot of the mountain. They entered and found Princess Sita lying in a pool of water. Her throat and stomach burned from Makara's venom. Son Vuong tried to help her sit up but she said it was too painful to move. Mi Nuong sat quietly by her side as Son Vuong explained how Sita swallowed the poison to protect living beings on both sides.

If she had not been the immortal daughter of Dragon Emperor, the amount of poison she swallowed would have killed her. As it was, it would take three months for the poison to leave her system. It was easier to heal the wounds of those whose skin was burned by the venom. Sita knew of a special medicinal balm that could heal the people's wounds in just seven days. She urged Son Vuong to find the mountain herbs and dragon saliva needed to mix the formula. Mi Nuong watched over Sita as her husband called to the birds to gather the herbs. He himself paid a visit to dragon friends beneath the sea, who were glad to give him some of their saliva in a small pot. When he returned, he simmered the herbs until they formed a thick paste to which he added the dragon saliva. The balm was wonderfully fragrant. He spread it on the wounds of all the people burned by Makara's venom and asked an old sea friend to distribute it to the sea creatures whose flesh had been burned.

Three months passed and Princess Sita recovered. Before she returned to the sea, she told Son Vuong and Mi Nuong, "Time was the only medicine that could heal my internal wounds. I am glad I

am better now or I would have been unable to bring the spring rains
to the people."

Knowing that Princess Sita was responsible for the gentle show-
ers that lightly dusted the trees and grasses every spring, Mi Nuong
was filled with an even greater regard for the dragon princess.

Princess Sita continued, "Be on your guard. Thuy Vuong will be
back, and every time he attacks, both sides will suffer. Thuy com-
mands the autumn and winter rains. He will use his power to create typhoons and floods. In his rage, he may again become Makara
and spit black venom. If that happens, I will have to assume my
dragon form and swallow the poison again."

Mi Nuong cried, "Is there no other way?"

Sita looked at her serenely. "There is no other way. I will become a dragon and swallow the venom. Every time I do, I will need three months to recover. Please, Brother and Sister, seek every way you can to protect the people. Son, you must show the people how to dig canals and build dams to keep out floodwaters and sea monsters. Do not hurl boulders at the sea creatures. If you and the people seek only to defend yourselves, the sea creatures will come to understand your intent. For my part, I will endeavor to create understanding and love among the sea creatures in the hope that hatred will one day dissolve and fighting between brothers cease."

Sita smiled as she turned towards Mi Nuong. "You, my sister, are a mortal, but through special efforts you can become immortal. Help others and study the Way."

The sea princess stood up and bid them farewell. "I must depart now. Thank you, Brother and Sister, for all your care these past months."

They accompanied Sita down the mountain until they came to a brook. Before stepping into the water, Sita reminded them, "Remember to make all your preparations before July to protect the people. And always remember to look upon all beings with the eyes of compassion."

She bent over and turned into a tiny pink fish that waved its tail good-bye before swimming from sight. Mi Nuong put her arm around Son Vuong, her eyes glistening with tears.

THE MISSION

VIET LIKED TO fish along the riverbanks like other village boys his age. One day, while fishing alone, he caught a small water snake that he released back into the river. The next bite turned out to be the same snake. Once again, he released it. When the snake bit his line a third time, he put it in his basket and secured the lid with a heavy stone.

He didn't have another bite all day. When evening shadows began to fall, he gathered up his belongings to return home. Suddenly remembering the snake, he opened the basket to let it go. To his surprise, the basket was empty. He couldn't imagine how the snake had managed to escape. He turned the basket upside down and shook it. Someone laughed behind him. He turned around, startled, and saw a boy his age with hair down to his shoulders. Viet asked him, "Who are you? What are you laughing at?"

The boy stopped laughing and said, "I am a son of Dragon Emperor. I was passing by and saw you. I wanted to make friends so I caught your attention by biting your line three times."

"You mean that little snake was you?" asked Viet.

"Yes, that little snake was me. I can change myself into a dragon, fish, or any other creature. Oh, look at all the stars in the sky! And there is such a refreshing breeze! Please don't go home yet. Let's sit here by the river and talk."

The boys sat in the grass by the river and talked about their different lives. "Do you know," asked Viet, "how much fun harvest time on land is? The fields are thick with golden rice plants. The villagers arrive early in the morning with sickles and carrying-yokes. As the sun shines, the people harvest the rice, laughing and talking the whole time. We form two teams and sing songs back and forth, inventing verses as we go. At noon, everyone sits beneath shady trees to eat lunch and rest. When evening falls, the villagers carry home their baskets, laden with rice, balanced on shoulder yokes."

Viet and the sea prince talked until the stars began to twinkle. Then the boys fell quiet and listened to the sounds of night. Viet said, "The crickets never stop chanting. Don't you wonder what they're trying to say?"

The sea prince looked surprised. "You mean you can't understand them?"

Viet shook his head. The sea prince nodded thoughtfully and said, "Yes, of course, there's no reason you should." Then he opened his mouth and out popped a small, bright jadestone. "Put this in your mouth and then listen to the crickets."

Viet placed the stone in his mouth. At first the crickets' cries seemed no different than usual, but then, suddenly, he found he could make out their words. He could even hear an occasional sound of clear, childlike laughter break the monotony of their chant. He listened to their excited buzz of conversation. The sea prince knew Viet understood by the smile on his face. He looked up and said, "Now try listening to the stars."

Viet looked up, wondering if the stars really talked to one another, too. He listened quietly and at first he felt as though he could understand them simply by looking at them. They twinkled sweet greetings. Then Viet could actually hear their voices. They called to him by name. A thousand conversations wove in and out of each other. Some stars talked about the Earth below, others talked about the two boys. Feeling somewhat self-conscious, Viet lowered his head and swallowed. In doing so, he accidentally swallowed the jadestone. He tried to cough it back up but without success. He felt terrible and turned to apologize to his new friend.

Before he could speak, the sea prince patted him on the shoulder and said, "No need to apologize. I know you swallowed the jadestone by accident. Perhaps it was meant to happen. From now on you will be able to understand the languages of all beings. Don't worry about me. I'll have another stone in a year. Cheer up! All I ask is that you never tell anyone about our meeting here tonight. It is very late and I must return to the sea palace. I'm sure you should be heading home, too. Perhaps we'll meet again one day."

From that day on Viet made tremendous progress in his studies. He only needed to hear a lesson once to have it memorized. He excelled at foreign languages. As he grew older, he loved to visit the capital, Phong Chau, in order to meet and talk with foreign merchants. They were all astonished at how quickly he mastered their native tongues.

Viet was chosen by his district's members to visit King Hung and pay him special respects on their behalf. Seeing how intelligent and conscientious Viet was, the king appointed him governor of Viet's home province and even renamed the province after him, calling it Viet Thuong.

Viet devoted his talents to bringing prosperity and happiness to the people in his province. Assisted by many able workers whom he personally selected from among the local people, agriculture and commerce flourished in the province, and merchants came from all over to trade their goods.

One day a Chinese merchant confided to Viet that he had been informed that the Chu dynasty was planning to invade Van Lang. He said, "One of the emperor's advisors has persuaded him that Van Lang is an uncivilized land in need of Chinese rule. But from what I've seen, although the culture of Van Lang differs from our own, your people enjoy peace and prosperity. You should use your position to find some way to prevent the impending war that can only bring untold suffering to both our peoples."

Viet thanked the merchant. Rather than heading at once to Phong Chau to discuss the matter with King Hung, he went down to the river and carefully thought the situation over. The best method to avert war might be to speak directly to Emperor Chu and help him see that war would only bring death and destruction to both sides. The emperor would have to be convinced that Van Lang enjoyed a rich culture of its own and was not in need of being civilized from the outside. Who should meet with the emperor of China? Should Viet offer to make the journey himself?

At that moment, a flock of white birds flew overhead. Their wings cut a graceful design against the blue sky. They were the loveliest birds Viet had ever seen. He heard the birds' leader call to the others, telling them to land near Viet. The birds sat in a circle around him. Their leader perched on his shoulder. Viet asked her, "Can you help me in my dilemma?"

She answered, "Yes indeed. We have been sent by Goddess Au Co to assist you. She agrees that you must undertake a diplomatic mission to Emperor Chu."

Viet said, "China is far away—how long will it take to get there?"

The birds giggled, and their leader said, "You will arrive as soon as you arrive."

Viet smiled. It was most pleasant speaking with these light-hearted birds. Like small children, they spoke without artifice or formality.

Their leader said, "We have just flown across the sea. Many merchant ships are now raising their sails and heading north. The winds are favorable. Now is the best time to make your journey. Goddess Au Co told us to urge you to make haste. You know many languages, including the language of Chu. You will be able to speak directly to Emperor Chu."

"But I haven't even begun preparations! I'll need all kinds of precious gifts to offer the emperor—gold, silver, ivory. I must ask King Hung's assistance in this."

The white bird spoke softly, "Explain the purpose of your mission to the king and then waste no time in making your departure. You'll need no more than a small amount of gold to cover traveling expenses. We will fly before your ship the length of the voyage. You can give two of us as a gift to Emperor Chu. That will suffice."

"Won't that seem rather a small gift for one kingdom to offer another?" asked Viet.

"A gift's value depends on its rarity. The empire of Chu has no lack of gold, silver, and ivory. Emperor Chu is a man of great learning and refinement. He will judge you more by your bearing and speech than by any gifts you bring. Our kind of bird is found only in Van Lang. We have never been seen in Chu. I am sure we will please the emperor."

Viet thanked the birds and returned home with two of them perched on his shoulders. The next morning he selected six strong, handsome, learned men to accompany him. First they went to Phong Chau and conferred with King Hung, who gladly sanctioned their mission and supplied them with provisions needed for their voyage. They didn't require much—some extra clothes, fresh water, food, a small amount of gold. They boarded a northbound merchant ship that made great speed thanks to favorable winds. The white birds were always overhead except for the two that remained faithfully perched on Viet's shoulders. They sailed for nearly a month, stopping now and then in small ports to replenish food and water. The birds would disappear at such times, reappearing high overhead as soon as the ship set sail again.

At long last they reached the shores of China, but it was now necessary to travel a great distance by land in order to reach the capital. They purchased seven horses for the month-long journey and slept at small inns along the way.

Viet used this time to talk to innkeepers and guests to familiarize himself with the customs and culture of Chu. Viet learned that Emperor Chu was both a scholar and philosopher who was working on a series of philosophical treatises left uncompleted by the former emperor. He learned that the emperor himself created the music and rituals used for such ceremonies as weddings and funerals. The music and customs of Chu were highly formalized, unlike those of Van Lang. No one in Chu offered areca nuts at weddings or social gatherings. Nor did they organize outdoor dances at which everyone was an equal participant. In Chu sharp divisions existed between the emperor and his subjects, teachers and students, parents and children. In Van Lang the people felt close to their king and greeted him with a simple bow like everyone else. A prince in Van Lang could dance and sing with the people. Parents and children sang together. But not so in Chu.

At last Viet and his companions reached the capital. Though they were offered a place to stay in the palace guest house, they chose instead to stay at a small private inn. They bedded down for a good night's sleep in order to be refreshed for their morning audience with the emperor.

Everyone slept soundly except for Viet, who was deep in thought. He knew the emperor was a man of great learning and he would have to choose his words well. Van Lang depended on their mission to avoid war. Viet had to find a way to convince the emperor not to send troops to colonize Van Lang.

Viet finally drifted off to sleep. When he awoke, sunlight streamed in through the window. He summoned the others to ready themselves. The two white birds perched on his shoulders.

Much more formal ceremony was observed at Emperor Chu's palace than at the palace of their own King Hung. Nonetheless, the Van Lang delegates appeared relaxed and confident. Viet greeted every person they met, whether a high official or simple guard, with the same respectful bow. At last they stood before the emperor's throne. Viet, folding his arms across his chest, bowed. He did not prostrate himself like the emperor's attendants. He said, "Your Majesty, please allow us to greet you according to the custom of Van Lang."

Viet chose to speak in his native tongue in order to show pride in his own culture. His voice echoed in the palace hall, clear as a bell. The emperor did not know the language of Van Lang. He turned to his advisors but they all shook their heads. One said, "Please, Your Majesty, allow me to summon an interpreter."

Before long, the advisor returned with a man who was tall and dark. This man prostrated before the emperor and then greeted the Van Lang delegates according to the manner of Van Lang. It was clear he had lived in their country and was familiar with their customs.

Viet folded his arms across his chest and bowed again to the emperor, saying, "Please, Your Majesty, allow us to greet you according to the custom of Van Lang."

The tall man translated. The emperor smiled and nodded. He invited the delegates to be seated and then asked, "Where have you come from, and why have you brought two birds with you?"

Viet answered, "We hail from Viet Thuong province of Van Lang kingdom. When we learned this rare species of bird was not known in your empire, we decided to bring two of them to you to offer as a gift. Though our offering is most humble, it expresses the deepest sincerity of our king and people."

The emperor was impressed by Viet's bearing. He asked, "Can you explain why your country is called Van Lang?"

Viet answered, "Your Majesty, though our country is small, our king is peace-loving and our people industrious. The name of our country expresses our unique culture. 'Van' means bright and beautiful. 'Lang' means peace-loving and kind."

"I have heard that all the people in your land have two toes that are joined together. Is that so?"

"Your Highness, there are some people in our country who have two webbed toes, but most do not. During our long travels we have encountered other peoples with webbed toes, including some in your own kingdom."

"I have been told that your people tattoo dragons on their bodies. What is the purpose of such a custom?"

"Your Majesty, our people are the descendents of a heavenly goddess and the dragon emperor of the sea. The snow-white goddess bird and sea dragon are the symbols of our race. Fishermen believe that if they tattoo a dragon on their bodies, they will be protected from sea monsters."

Viet continued, "Your Majesty, our land is like a bridge between the cultures of east and west. Because many foreigners pass through our kingdom, many of our people are proficient in foreign tongues."

The emperor listened intently. He asked, "And what is your name?"

"Your Majesty, my name is Viet Thuong."

"How many family names exist in your country?"

"There are one hundred in all. Long ago Goddess Au Co and Dragon Emperor gave birth to the first one hundred children of our race. The names they gave them have been passed down through the generations as our family names. My own king, King Hung Vuong, honored me by naming my home province after me."

"One hundred family names. . . . Your population cannot be too small. . ."

Suddenly one of the emperor's advisors stood up. He was a man with a thin beard and pinched face. He addressed the emperor, "Your Majesty, Van Lang is a small, backward country. Look at how they cut their hair short and leave their heads uncovered. If you could see how they chew areca nuts you would know how primitive they are. Clearly they are in need of civilization."

No doubt, thought Viet, this advisor was responsible for the plot to invade Van Lang. Viet spoke, "Your Majesty, civilization takes many forms. North and South are different. Wearing long hair and hats in a tropical climate like ours would not be intelligent. Short hair is far more practical as we labor in our rice fields. We recognize that our bodies are a gift from the ancestors to be treated with respect, but we do not consider cutting our hair and nails an abuse of our bodies.

On the contrary, we consider it a better way to care for them. Among our people, dragon tattooing is a fine art form and a way to preserve our heritage while surrounded by people of other cultures."

"But why do you chew areca nuts?"

"Chewing the areca is a lovely and meaningful custom. The areca nut refreshes one's breath and brightens conversation at social gatherings. It is far preferable to smoking tobacco. You have never heard the story that explains the origin of the areca nut, thus it is difficult for you to understand its deep significance to us."

The emperor asked Viet to tell him the story and Viet began to recount the tale of Tan, Lang, and Thao in the emperor's own tongue. He explained how King Hung Vuong II initiated the custom of chewing areca nuts. Viet spoke so fluently and fervently that everyone in the hall was spellbound. The emperor was visibly moved.

"Your Majesty, not only does the areca nut freshen the breath, it also strengthens the teeth. People who chew areca rarely suffer toothaches. In our land, no gathering is considered complete without areca. If you ever paid a visit to our king, I am sure he would offer it to you."

The emperor smiled, "And at such a time I would have a chance to discover its merits myself. But let me ask you this—what purpose has brought you to Chu?"

Viet said, "We have heard that for three years your kingdom has suffered no drought or flood. Peace has flourished in all four directions and your people have prospered. Knowing that such fortune must be due to your virtue as emperor, we crossed mountains and rivers to pay our respects. We have seen for ourselves how you have brought peace, culture, and prosperity to your people. We are confident that such an emperor would not waste precious lives by fanning the flames of war. Though we do not have as many troops as your army, our king and people share one heart. We repelled the mighty army of An when it invaded our kingdom. It is our hope that you will extend your virtue to ensure long-lasting peace among all peoples."

The emperor answered, "Thank your king for sending you here and for offering these two rare, exquisite birds. I accept them but insist that any future delegations from your kingdom refrain from bringing gifts. What has our empire ever done for you that you should feel compelled to make offerings to us? It would be improper for me to expect tribute from your kingdom."

The emperor turned and spoke directly to the pinch-faced advisor. "There shall be no invasion of Van Lang. I want diplomatic ties instituted at once and maintained. Van Lang is a civilized land like our own."

The emperor looked at Viet and said, "Rest assured, I have understood your intent in coming here. Long ago, our first emperor decreed that we should never invade our southern neighbors. I will abide by the ancestors rather than be swayed by troublemakers."

The emperor ordered a horse-drawn carriage and map be given to the Van Lang mission. Though they hardly needed a map after having made the long journey successfully on their own, they did not refuse the emperor's kind gifts. Still, they smiled privately to themselves. With a young leader as capable as Viet and a flock of intelligent birds as escorts, what need had they for the emperor's map?

THE SPIRAL PALACE

KING THUC was unable to sleep. Impatiently he waited for daybreak, which would bring the promised River Messenger, the one who would help him complete his spiral-shaped palace fortress.

Construction on the palace had come to a halt after six months of catastrophe. Walls had collapsed time and again despite the best efforts of the kingdom's finest architects and builders. The idea and design for the unusual palace were the king's own, and he was determined to see it to completion. His architects shook their heads and said they could not go on. Such a palace could only be built by the gods. It was impossible to build walls as high as the king wanted. How would they haul the heavy stones? The king's plans were too ambitious. He envisioned fortress walls twisting like dragons up the steep hill, encircling a fine palace at the top which would command a sweeping view in all directions. He wanted the palace roof to spread out like the wings of a giant garuda bird.

The king's dream was bringing nothing but misery to his people. Hundreds of workers had been injured or killed while working on the project. The king turned a deaf ear to the people's cries. Many whispered that the angry spirits of those slain in the king's fight to usurp the throne from King Hung were responsible for the accidents; that to seek vengeance for their deaths they would not allow the king to complete his palace. Sometimes late at night, spine-tingling wails and moans could be heard at the foot of the hill. Some people claimed they heard the mournful plucking of a ghostly sitar by the river at night. Still others talked about the innkeeper's daughter who was possessed by a spirit. Day and night she shrieked and cursed the king. The innkeeper, terrified that her blasphemy would be reported to the king, kept her locked in a room by herself.

King Thuc had heard all these rumors but chose to ignore them. He had heard no wails of departed souls. One night, however, he was awakened by strains of mournful sitar music. The anguished tune made him uneasy, but he still did not believe in ghosts seeking vengeance. Nonetheless, he heeded the advice of his ministers and had a great altar built to invoke Dragon Emperor's aid.

The altar was soon finished and the king began to pray. Suddenly an old man with a long white beard appeared. He took a look at the half-completed fortress and shook his head. He said, "If you continue to build in this way, you are doomed to failure!"

The king asked, "Venerable Sir, can you explain why we are unable to complete the spiral palace?"

"This design is too intricate and ambitious for you to complete on your own. Tomorrow at daybreak, I will send River Messenger to help you."

The old man departed despite the king's pleas for him to stay longer.

Now the king could not sleep. Was that distant sound the sitar again? He rose from his bed and lit a lamp. He pushed aside a curtain and looked up at the stars shining in the cloudless sky. Strains of music, now louder, drifted toward the window from the river. The sad sounds conjured up an image in the king's mind of hands desperately trying to clutch at something. Then the music faded until it was no more than a whisper mingling with the night breeze and crickets' chant. Suddenly he heard a clang of swords and a noise like crashing bricks and stones. He held his head in his hands and shook it as if to rid his ears of the disturbing sounds.

Weary, he leaned against a screen and found his thoughts drifting back to simpler times. He remembered his youth when his father had been an acquaintance of King Hung XVIII. A closer friendship did not develop between the king and his father due to the great difference between their personalities. King Hung XVIII had been a jovial, friendly man. His father, it must be admitted, was vain and longed for power.

Thuc's father wished to ask for the king's beautiful daughter in marriage to Thuc and sent a servant to convey his wishes. The king responded by laughing and saying, "Tell your master that if he wishes to ask for my daughter's hand in marriage to his son, he must come and speak to me directly! I can't decide such an important matter through an intermediary."

Thuc's father considered the king's response an affront to his pride. He felt deeply insulted and allowed his anger to poison his heart. He plotted to overthrow King Hung and began to build a secret army. When he learned that King Hung XVIII had given his daughter in marriage to the mountain god Son Vuong, he decided it was time to strike the capital. Before he could summon his army, however, he fell deathly ill. He called his son to his deathbed and made his last request, "Son, I depend on you to lead our troops to victory against the king. Avenge your father's honor!"

Thuc obeyed his father's last wish and mounted an attack.

King Hung had placed too much faith in Son Vuong and Dragon Emperor to defend the throne for him. His own defensive preparations were too weak to withstand attack. Because the rebellion took place in July, the people's strength was already wasted by the floods that resulted from the battle between Son Vuong and his brother Thuy Vuong. Son Vuong, trapped in the mountains, was unable to bring relief soon enough to King Hung. Faced with certain defeat and over-come with grief, King Hung drowned himself by jumping into a well.

Thuc declared himself king and replaced the former court with members of his own clan. It took eight more months of fighting, however, to wipe out the many pockets of resistance. The new king had to dispel rumors that he was a foreign invader. He had to con-vince the people that he, too, was a descendent of Au Co and Dragon Emperor and would continue to observe the traditions long cher-ished by the people of Van Lang.

Because every blade of grass and every leaf in Phong Chau held memories of the long reign of the Hung clan, King Thuc selected a new site for his capital in the district of Phong Khe. He envisioned a mighty spiralling palace fortress on a great hill to herald a new era.

A cock's crow called King Thuc back to the moment. It was dawn. He washed his face and changed clothes and waited in his reception quarters. Before long, an attendant entered to announce the arrival of River Messenger. "Your Majesty, when mists still clung to the water, we saw a golden turtle swim toward shore. He spoke the language of humans and introduced himself as River Messenger. He turned himself into an old man with a long white beard."

The king asked that River Messenger be escorted to his chambers at once. He invited the old man to be seated on the royal couch.

River Messenger spoke, "I am Kim Quy, chief assistant to Dragon Emperor. He asked me to come assist you. Put all your worries aside. Your spiral fortress shall be completed. Now, show me your efforts thus far."

The king led Kim Quy to the hill. Although rubble from collapsed walls was piled everywhere, there were enough portions of the walls remaining to give Kim Quy a sense of the king's design. He examined it most carefully, now and again shaking his head and mumbling something to himself. At last, he looked at the king and said, "You have undertaken an enormous project. Your design is an inspired one, but you have caused the people too much suffering. You must not force so great a burden on the people."

The king said, "I am afraid that if I do not complete the palace after all this work, the new dynasty's reputation will be at stake."

"I have been thinking the same thing. Therefore, I intend to help you, but in a way that will conserve the energies of the people while completing the fortress just as you have envisioned it. Please arrange a meeting for me with your master builders."

The meeting was arranged without delay right at the foot of the hill. Kim Quy used a chopstick to draw diagrams in the dirt and met at length with the master builders. They walked up the hill, stopping at every interval where walls had collapsed. Kim Quy walked back and forth, taking measurements and pointing out details with a stick. Among other things, he showed them how to design a more effective shoulder yoke for carrying supplies. It was dark before they were finished.

The king had dinner waiting when Kim Quy returned to his quarters. Kim Quy said, "Your Majesty, send half the workers home to their farms and villages, where they are needed by their families. Provide them with ample supplies of food, clothing, and medicine in exchange for their hard work. The remaining workers will be enough to complete the fortress."

In addition to paying the workers, the king followed Kim Quy's counsel and organized a special offering to the spirits of all those who had died in the rebellion and while working on the palace. Monks and village elders from throughout the kingdom were invited to attend. A great altar was heaped with platters of rice, sweet potatoes, and other dishes. During the fourteen days of offerings, the food was also distributed to the poor along with clothing and medicine.

On the seventh day, Kim Quy asked the king to go with him to visit an area called Thet Dieu. When night fell, they wanted to stay in a local inn. The innkeeper was afraid to let them enter.

"Your Majesty," he said, "ghosts haunt this humble tavern. It is not possible to have a quiet night's rest here. I would be honored to offer you a meal, but please find another place to sleep."

The king replied, "We are not afraid of ghosts," and insisted on staying the night.

The king and Kim Quy were shown to the room next to that of the innkeeper's daughter. At midnight, a violent banging began at their door, accompanied by bloodcurdling shouts and screams. The king was sure that no young girl could make such a horrible disturbance on her own. Kim Quy poked his head out the window and shouted, "Disturb this place no more!" But the racket did not cease. The window shutters rattled and shook. Kim Quy, enlisting his magical powers, tossed sparks of fire at the window, creating a barrier of light through which no phantom could pass. Still, the banging and screaming lasted all night. Only at the first cock's crow did it cease. Kim Quy and the king ran outside to see if they could catch a glimpse of the intruders, but all they saw was a streak of blue light disappearing behind a nearby mountain.

That day the king ordered an exploration of the mountain. A mass grave was discovered, heaped with human bones and a broken sitar. It was obvious that a mass execution had taken place during the war. The bones and sitar were placed in coffins and brought back to the foot of the great altar. For seven days, people came to weep and pay their respects to all those who had perished during the rebellion. The innkeeper came as well, reporting how his daughter had suddenly fallen unconscious after the bones were placed in coffins. When he ran to lift her up, she acted like one who has just woken from a long nightmare. Though a little weak, she was her normal self again, no longer possessed by a tormented spirit.

The bones were cremated in a solemn ceremony. Incense and sandalwood were thrown onto the fire as people prayed. As the flames licked the air, a white bird flew forth from the fire and disappeared into the white clouds.

Kim Quy counseled the king on how best to run a kingdom. "Remember," he said, "that a country belongs to all its people. Unless hatred is eased, the people cannot prosper. Always be an example to your people. Respect and protect their lives. Let no one die unjustly. Do not oppress the people. Only thus may bloodshed be prevented. Be an example of peace and harmony to the people. If you live in peace and harmony, so will they."

The king took Kim Quy's counsel to heart. He even took a new

name, An Duong, which meant "Radiant Example of Peace," in order
to be constantly reminded of his role and responsibilities. He
renamed the kingdom "Au Lac" to show his reverence for their goddess ancestor.

The king spent several months traveling throughout the kingdom.
He distributed goods to the poor and ordered the release of all pris-
oners of war. The people's feelings toward him softened, especially
when they learned he had received support from Dragon Emperor.
The king saw that the poor received land, the hungry were fed, and
that the people had the tools they needed to carry on their trades.
He provided fishermen with nets and weavers with yarn. He listened to the grievances of the people wherever he went and did all
within his power to bring about justice.

When he returned to Phong Khe in late summer, he was astonished to find his spiral palace fortress completed. He gazed at it,
speechless. There before him rose the palace of his dreams. At the
hill's pinnacle, the palace roof spread out like the wings of a mighty
garuda. Designs of garuda birds and dancing goddesses embellished
the palace walls. Diamond-shaped windows were cut into the walls
affording views of the surrounding countryside. King An Duong
found Kim Quy waiting for him by the entrance gate.

Kim Quy said, "Your Majesty, the palace fortress is completed. It
is time for me to bid you farewell."

The king begged Kim Quy to stay longer, but he declined. "There
is much work awaiting me beneath the sea."

The king, unable to conceal the disappointment in his voice, said,
"I have not had a chance to repay even a small part of your kindness. You have shown me that the people and I must be as one. So
many tasks await our kingdom! The palace is completed, and now
I must turn my attention to more pressing matters. There is talk of
an invasion from the north. Can you offer me any guidance?"

Kim Quy answered, "Peace or danger depends on the merit of a country's king. If you set an example of virtue, you need never fear insurrection. As for foreign invasion, all rulers must be prepared for such attacks. I will leave you something to help you defend your kingdom."

Kim Quy bent down and cut a sliver off one of his toenails. It grew into the size of a bow. He showed it to the king and said, "This is a magic crossbow. Watch." Kim Quy pointed the bow at a tall tree. There was a sound like a deep bell vibrating. Within seconds all the leaves fell off the tree. "In the event foreign troops invade Au Lac, you need only point this bow at them and they will be dispersed immediately."

The king accompanied Kim Quy to the river, where he turned back into a golden turtle and, nodding farewell, disappeared into the water. King An Duong returned to his new palace with the magic crossbow, pleased that he now possessed the means to protect his kingdom.

❦BLOOD PEARLS

NEWS THAT troops from the neighboring kingdom of Trieu had crossed the northeastern border of Au Lac plunged the people into panic. Princess Thanh Chau was certain the news was false. Surely the invading troops were from the kingdom of Tan and not from Trieu, the kingdom of her beloved husband. She remembered how six months earlier, shortly before her husband, Trong Thuy, returned to visit his homeland, he told her how worried he was that Tan might invade Au Lac at any moment. He said, "In the event the Tan army invades, our two kingdoms must join forces to repel them. If the invasion takes place before my return, how will I know where to find you? In the confusion, you may be forced to flee the capital."

Thanh Chau thought for a moment and then said, "I understand that if Tan invades our two countries, it will be necessary for you to remain with your army to fight. When you return to Au Lac to find me, follow the path marked by goose feathers from my cloak. I will pluck several feathers from my feathered cloak and place them at every crossroad I pass to indicate which road I have taken."

King An Duong did not share his daughter's belief that the invaders were from Tan. He said, "Tan has not recovered from the last war.

Their new dynasty is still too weak and disorganized to plan the invasion of another country. I never suspected your husband could be so treacherous. The reconciliation between our two countries after the last war, symbolized by your marriage, has turned out to be no more than part of a plot to ruin our kingdom. With all my heart, I regret that I ever allowed you to wed the prince of Trieu."

With the entire country of Au Lac convinced that Trieu was invading, the princess knew it was futile to try to convince her father otherwise. But she knew that her husband could never betray them. No one knew him better than she. She knew he considered Au Lac a second home. He had no reason to cause trouble between their two kingdoms. Furthermore, why would he destroy the rare and beautiful relationship he shared with her?

In any case, Trong Thuy was well aware that his father's kingdom was no match for Au Lac in war. His father, Trieu Da, had already been defeated in his attempt to conquer Au Lac, thanks to King An Duong's magic bow that could disperse entire armies. It was because of that very bow that King Trieu Da signed a treaty with King An Duong, pledging peaceful relations. To show his sincerity, King Trieu Da even suggested his son marry King An Duong's daughter. Because King An Duong desired stable and harmonious relations between the two kingdoms, he agreed, but only on the condition that his son-in-law follow the old customs of Au Lac and live with his bride's family for three years. In the happy atmosphere of restored peace, the wedding lifted the people's hopes and spirits. In the capital and countryside, people hung lanterns and flower garlands to celebrate the union of their princess with the prince of Trieu. The festivities lasted three days and nights.

Although Princess Thanh Chau was at first a little shy and nervous, she soon fell in love with the handsome young prince. He was an accomplished, cultured young man and expressed deep and tender love for the princess. They seemed a perfect match. People surrounded their carriage wherever they went and tossed flowers to the young couple. Sometimes the carriage could barely move forward, the crowds were so thick. The prince loved to travel throughout the kingdom and so they took many excursions. Thanh Chau noticed how her husband jotted down notes wherever they went. She did not ask him what he was writing. No doubt, he was recording all their happy moments to share as precious memoirs in the future.

A year passed. One day King Trieu Da sent letters to both King An Duong and his son. He said he missed his son and wanted him to return home for a six-month visit. Thanh Chau could tell how torn her husband felt. He wanted to obey his father's wishes but he was most reluctant to leave her behind. He suggested she join him. She would then have a chance to see his home. The princess was delighted with the idea and so was most disappointed when her father refused. He gave the excuse that the period of three years had not yet passed, and so he could not allow Thanh Chau to follow her husband. Thanh Chau knew that her father's real reason was that he could not bear the thought of her being absent even for a few months. The couple pleaded with him three times, but each time his answer was no.

As the day for her husband's departure neared, Thanh Chau grew ever more sad. Her tears fell like rain, and Trong Thuy hesitated over whether or not he should go. But on the appointed day, he and his attendants mounted their steeds and began their journey home. He looked back and saw Thanh Chau standing in the palace courtyard, looking as forlorn as a weeping willow.

When, several months later, news of the invasion reached King An Duong, he exclaimed, "Can it be King Trieu Da no longer fears my magic crossbow?" Confident he could not lose the war, King An

Duong laughed and sipped a glass of wine. News of fierce, bloody battles soon reached the capital, however. The invaders were advancing like a hurricane, leaving death and destruction in their wake. When a scout arrived with the news that the invaders were closing in on the capital, the king knew it was time to take out the magic bow and face the enemy. He dressed in full battle attire and mounted his steed.

The invading troops poured into Phong Khe like waves of a stormy sea. They broke through Au Lac's lines of defense as if they were no more than sticks of bamboo. The Trieu troops carried thick straw shields that could not be pierced by the arrows of Au Lac's soldiers. When Au Lac sent in ground troops, Trieu countered by sending in their cavalry. The northern half of the capital quickly fell to the enemy.

King An Duong galloped into the fray and prepared to raise his magic bow against the invaders, confident they would soon be dispersed by the bow's powerful magic. One aim of the bow and the soldiers would be scattered by thousands of arrows flying as quickly as lightning bolts. He raised the bow. Nothing happened. He raised it again. Still nothing. The bow no longer possessed magical powers. It was no more than a giant turtle's toenail.

King An Duong cried in despair, "It is over!"

He turned his horse and sped back to the palace. There he found Thanh Chau standing in the courtyard clutching her cloak of white goose feathers. The king hoisted her up behind him on the horse's back and said, "The invaders are closing in. We must flee. Hold on to me tightly."

Off they galloped, leaving the palace behind and soon passing beyond the capital's southern gate. Before long, it was nightfall. Swifter than the wind, the horse carried them through dark forests. The road seemed no more than a blur. Thanh Chau's loosened hair flew wildly

in the wind, and she longed for daylight. Throughout the night, however, she pulled feathers from her cloak to strew on the trail behind
them. At last, the pink glow of dawn began to disperse the darkness, and the stars faded one by one.

King An Duong was suddenly startled by the thunderous sound
of galloping horses pursuing them. He turned around but saw nothing save for a few white feathers hanging in the wind. He dug his
heels into the horse's flanks and raced towards the reddening horizon.

Princess Thanh Chau was seized with a sudden, terrible doubt.
Who could be pursuing them? No one but her husband would know
to follow the path of white feathers. But if Tan had invaded, Trong
Thuy would be engaged in battle and certainly not looking for her
this soon. Her heart sank, and she understood that she had been
betrayed.

Sickened, she remembered how Trong Thuy had once said, "If Tan
invades, our two kingdoms must defend ourselves. Our cavalry are
second to none. But how will Au Lac defend itself?"

The princess had smiled and said, "There is no need to worry
about Au Lac. My father has a magic crossbow from the River God
Kim Quy. He needs only to aim it at enemy troops to instantly disperse them."

Trong Thuy's face had lit up as he said, "Magnificent! But have
you ever seen that magic bow yourself? Have you ever held it?"

"I have indeed. I know where my father keeps it safely hidden. I
would be glad to show it to you."

Trong Thuy declined. "Of course, I would love to see it, but it
would not be proper for you to disturb something that belongs to
your father."

The princess laughed. "What belongs to my father belongs to me.
Wait here and I will fetch it."

When she returned, she held the magic bow. Trong Thuy examined it with great interest and then handed it back, telling her to
return it at once. A month later, he asked her if he might see it again.
This time the king was gone on business for three days, and the
princess suggested her husband keep it in his own chambers overnight
if he would like to examine it more carefully.

Now the princess understood that her husband had either damaged the magic bow or replaced it with a fake. How could she have
been so misled? Her thoughts were interrupted as she realized the
king's horse had come to an abrupt halt. They were at the edge of
the sea with nowhere else to flee. The rising sun stained the waters
blood red. They could hear the horses of their pursuers closing in
on them.

King An Duong looked up at the sky and out over the sea. In
anguish, he cried, "Mother and Father, have you abandoned us? Kim
Quy, where are you now?"

A golden turtle emerged from the waves and said, "Quick, the
enemy is at your back!"

King An Duong turned around and saw Trieu horsemen emerg-
ing from the forest, raising a blinding storm of dust and dirt. But the
princess, in her sad confusion, believed he was looking at her. Yes,
she thought, by placing her trust in someone who was false, she had
caused her country's downfall. She said, "Father, if it was my intention to betray you, let my dead body turn to dust. Otherwise, may
my drops of blood turn to precious gems to prove my heart was
ever faithful to you and our people."

She seized her father's sword and stabbed herself. It happened too
quickly for King An Duong to prevent it. Her lifeless body fell from
the horse.

Kim Quy shouted again, "Hurry, the enemy is upon you!"

King An Duong jumped from his horse and embraced his daughter. Tears streamed down his cheeks. Kim Quy pulled him away and parted the waters to reveal an escape path for the king, a path which led to the sea palace below. The waters closed back over them.

The pursuers reached the shore. Trong Thuy, dressed in black armor, jumped from his horse. King An Duong had disappeared. Only his horse stood by the lapping waves. Suddenly, the prince saw his wife's body. Her blood flowed over the sand into the sea. He cried her name and gathered her in his arms. Her body was already cold, but her face was serene. Trong Thuy could not hold back his tears. He carried her body back to Phong Khe on his horse and buried her in the courtyard of the spiral palace.

King Trieu Da conquered Au Lac. He joined the two kingdoms and gave them the name Nam Viet. But his son refused to have anything more to do with him. All day, Trong Thuy sat alone in the places he had once sat with his beloved wife. He remembered how she enjoyed looking at the moon, how she washed her face and changed her clothes. He recalled all their happy times together. Unable to bear his grief any longer, he jumped into the palace well and drowned himself.

King Trieu moved the capital to Phien Ngung and took a new name for himself, Trieu Vu.

Not long after that, fishermen in Chau Dien district discovered pearls tucked in the hearts of oysters that had tasted drops of Princess Thanh Chau's blood. It was said that if you rinsed the pearls in water from the well where Prince Trong Thuy drowned himself, the pearls cast a brilliant and penetrating light. People still tell the story of the young couple, expressing regret that the prince betrayed his love's trust.

A BOUQUET OF WILDFLOWERS

MANY YEARS AGO, the wife of a good-natured farmer passed away after giving birth to their second child. The farmer raised the children alone until, when his son was sixteen and his daughter eleven, he too fell ill and died. Following his last request, the children buried him in one of their rice paddies, surrounded by o-moi and so-dua trees.

The children knew that six generations ago, one of their ancestors, a scholar who wanted to flee his difficult career, had moved south from central Vietnam, cleared a forested area, and established four fertile rice fields. For six generations, his children and their children worked hard and became real farmers.

Before his death, the farmer called his two children to his deathbed and made this last request: "After I die, do not sell any of our rice fields. Take care of them and continue to plant and to harvest. You know that for five generations, our ancestors have believed that a treasure of gold and jewels was buried by the founder of this land somewhere in our fields, but so far, no one has found it. Our ancestors left a poem, and my father was told this poem would help us find the buried treasure. But for several generations, no one has under-stood the meaning of the poem. Your grandfather told me that to uncover the meaning of the poem, one must contemplate it for a long time. During your grandfather's lifetime, our country went through many adversities, and he had to move often as a refugee, although he always returned to the land. Other houses fell in ruins, but your grandfather had worked hard to rebuild and maintain our house. Grandfather never had time to reflect upon the poem and he asked me to find the time to meditate on it. But I have not had the time to do it either; I have only been able to work in the fields.

"So I pass the treasure and these instructions on to you. Don't be as busy as I have been. Work just enough to live, and take the time to find the deep meaning of the poem and uncover the treasure. That will be the best way for you to show your gratitude to our ances-tors. The poem is on page forty-four of the family register, which is in the wooden case on the ancestors' altar."

The day after their father's funeral, the brother and sister pros-trated before the altar and took down the family register. Ceremo-niously, with great respect, they opened the register to page forty-four and read the poem:

> No tile roof above
> no land to settle below.
> Don a new robe
> and tread forward with your staff.
> With just one step, the world will tremble
> like a dragon leaping on its prey.

Brother and Sister sat still for a long time. Their incense stick had almost burned to the end before the young lady's voice broke the silence, "Brother, do you understand? The poem sounds wonderful, but I don't understand a word."

The brother did not reply. He just closed the family register and put it back in the wooden case on the altar, respectfully. Then the two of them prostrated before the ancestors again. After several minutes more, the brother said, "Grandfather was right. We will need a lot of time to understand. Let us do as we were told. After we settle down, we must carve out time to meditate on that poem."

Time went by quickly. For six years, Brother and Sister had excellent crops, and they were able to rebuild their ancestors' house. The tile roof was shiny-red. In the yard, the jackfruit trees grew green and dense, laden with fruit. The rice granary was always full. Two strong water buffaloes shared the plowing to break up the ebony soil of the rice fields and allow the young green rice plants to grow. Brother and Sister were very successful and very generous, and the people of the village loved and respected them both. When someone needed to borrow rice, they always received more than they asked for. Everyone who worked for them was honest, treating their masters' property as their own.

The young ladies of the village all had eyes for the young man, but the thought of marrying never occurred to him. In fact, he was determined not to get married so he would have time to look deeply into the poem. When his sister came to marriage age, the young men in the village all courted her. She was beautiful and compassionate, and many intermediaries came to propose marriage. But she always refused. She too wanted to have time to penetrate the meaning of the poem.

But the two of them were too busy in their daily work to have enough time to contemplate anything. Not that they had any debts, or major repairs, or farm problems. Their many workers helped with the house and the fields, and their crops flourished. It was just that the time went by so fast.

Finally, the brother began to have sleepless nights worrying about all of this. He was taking good care of the rice fields and the house inherited from his ancestors, but he did not feel happy. He could not feel peaceful until he had found the deep meaning of the poem. Why? Did he really need his ancestors' treasure? He already had success and riches, yet the very source of that success—the house, the garden, the rice fields—were obstacles to his search. There were only twenty-four hours in a day, and those hours were completely filled. At dawn, he ate breakfast and went to work in the fields. At noon, he had a light lunch and a nap. In the afternoon, he continued working in the fields with the buffaloes. And in the evening, there was only time for washing, eating, and sleeping. When would he ever have time to contemplate?

If he were without his house and rice fields, he would be just a homeless wanderer. But with a house and rice fields, he had time only for them. He tossed and turned all night, thinking of the hermits of old who had left their homes and gone into the remote jungle to seek the Way. Yes, to have time, he thought, I may have to leave everything behind. But how can I leave the fortune inherited from our ancestors? The treasure is in the rice fields. To leave would be to lose everything.

Time continued. When he was thirty years old, the brother's aspiration to understand the poem had only grown deeper. His fields were thick with golden rice and the harvesters talked, laughed, and sang joyfully as they worked. During moonlit evenings at threshing time, young men and women gathered and sang together. But none of these things made him happy. His sister noticed this and offered to take complete charge of the house and all the field chores, so he could devote himself to studying the poem.

Her idea seemed wise, but to put it into practice was not easy. Even after his sister had begun to take care of everything inside and outside, he could not remain idle. He was too accustomed to working, and he felt unhappy when his hands were free from chores. He realized that he would need to leave home and find a remote temple if he really wanted to contemplate the poem.

So he did. He left home and went to a remote region of central Vietnam, where he was accepted at a temple. During his retreat there, his sister sent five hundred pounds of rice every month to the temple as a donation. Undistracted by chores, the brother was finally free to meditate on the poem.

Three years passed. Now the young man walked slowly on the sunny, deserted village road back to his farm. He had not seen anyone yet. When he got to the crossroads, he put down his bag and sat in the shade of an old banyan tree. Everything was completely still.

For three years he had worked in the monastic community planting potatoes, cleaning vegetables, chopping wood, and carrying water. At the temple, hard work was very much a part of the practice. In fact, he worked harder than he had at home, but somehow he also had time to memorize each line of the poem. He recited it silently countless times during sitting meditation, walking meditation, and work. But even after three years, nothing had been revealed. The first two sentences seemed to be the most mysterious:

> No tile roof above
> no land to settle below.

Where was this place? Could it be a pond? No, a pond still had "land to settle below." And how could there be a pond in the rice fields? There was only the duckweed pond, and that was in the backyard. Besides, how could a treasure be buried in a pond? Perhaps the treasure was under a large stone? But there were no large stones in the fields either. The place where there is no tile roof must be the open air, he thought. He felt he finally understood the first line.

However, he was not at all sure about the second line and even more unclear about the next two:

> Don a new robe
> and tread forward with your staff.

This must refer to his ancestors' burial site, he thought. These lines suggested a funeral: people putting on mourning robes, a monk holding a staff. But his ancestors' tombs were in the village cemetery, not in the rice fields. In the field surrounded by o-moi and so-dua trees, there were only his parents' tombs. The final two lines confused him the most:

> With just one step, the world will tremble
> like a dragon leaping on its prey.

He thought of geomancy. Perhaps a good geomancer would be able to locate the "dragon's mouth" in the four rice fields. But how could there be a blue dragon or a white tiger in such a vast, flat area?

At the temple, he had once given the poem to a venerable monk and asked him to explain it, but the old monk could not help at all. After three years at the temple, the young man felt he did not have much better an understanding of the poem than when he had arrived there. But his mind and spirit had changed. He looked at things more attentively and somehow began to feel a connection between his daily life of eating, sleeping, and working, and his ancestors' poem. His life and the poem felt as close as the blood circulating in his body.

The rays of the sun lengthened, and the afternoon air became cooler. The young man stood up, put his bag back on his shoulder, and continued walking. The rice plants surrounding him were tender and green, and they waved to him in the afternoon breeze. A light happiness permeated his whole being. Suddenly, the sound of singing caught his attention. He stopped to listen, and he heard a voice as joyful as the young rice plants swaying in the breeze. The voice grew clearer and clearer, and the man recognized it as his sister's. Feeling as excited as the New Year, he ran ahead looking for his sister, and he saw her walking up from the mulberry field singing to the water buffaloes, a bouquet of wildflowers in her hand. When she caught sight of her brother, she ran toward him and spontaneously handed him the wildflowers she had picked in the field. Smiling widely, she looked him over from head to toe, at his brown clothes and the gray bag on his shoulder. Then she looked directly into his eyes. Her gaze was as clear as a fresh stream, bringing comfort and peace to his whole body and mind. His sorrows suddenly vanished, and he felt as light as a floating cloud. She was his sister, but the look in her eyes was as generous and protective as a mother's.

Brother and Sister drove the herd down to the meadow and sat on a mound of earth beneath a cool shade tree. Then he began to tell her about his three years of temple life and his insights about the poem, and she listened attentively, without interrupting him or missing a single detail. When he finished, he looked deeply at his sister. Her skin was tanned, her body healthy, her eyes bright, and her smile fresh and compassionate. She used to be somewhat quiet. Now she was completely silent. When he saw her manner and the look in her eyes, he knew she had found peace, joy, and happiness.

She understood his mind, and she said, "After you left, I took care of the house and the fields alone, but I didn't consider it a burden. I felt completely at ease doing all the chores. I did them slowly, and I enjoyed it. You were always able to plow the fields in seven days; it took me twelve. I realized that whether I finished quickly or slowly, it would come to the same end. Whenever I held the plow and pushed the buffalo forward, I thought, "This might be where the treasure is buried." Realizing that any spot in the field might be the place where the treasure was buried, I plowed even more slowly, giving my full care and attention to each inch of soil.

"On the afternoon of the eighth day, while plowing the last furrow in the field close to the pagoda, I realized that in all four fields, every spot is a treasure! The treasure is not hidden in the soil. It is each inch of the land itself. I saw that the land is precious not just because it produces rice, but because it is the land. I looked at the plow, the buffalo, the white clouds, the sky, and the plumeria trees behind the pagoda and I saw that the plow is precious because it's a plow, and the buffalo is precious because it's a buffalo, and the clouds are precious because they are clouds, and the plumeria trees are precious because they are plumeria trees. I realized that what we have been looking for is not one particular treasure, but the unique presence of all beings in the universe, including ourselves.

"I felt happier than if I had discovered a treasure chest. I walked home after a day's work in the fields. I felt an enormous love for all life and all beings. The next day and the three days that followed, as I plowed, my mind was very clear. I could see that each drop of my sweat was nothing less than my entire soul watering the soil. I realized that I am not any more important than the buffalo or anything else.

"If I had been able to write, I would have written to you to let you know that whether or not you found the meaning of the poem or discovered the treasure, our lives would be filled with happiness. I continued to send rice to your temple each month, hoping that you would be inspired to find the meaning of the poem for its own sake and not just for finding our ancestors' treasure.

"What would we do with the treasure anyway if we found it? Would we buy more land? Build more houses? Aren't our four fields enough for us to plow? And who would take care of the houses? This house and fields were already enough to make you take refuge in the temple.

"I have no wish for the treasure. But I know that there is something in the poem of our ancestors that is deeply connected to our lives. Since the first time you read it to me, I've repeated the words many times, without comprehending the meaning at all. Still, each time I read it, my heart pounds as when I hear the wind blowing between the so-dua leaves. I don't know what the wind is trying to say. I only know that I enjoy its sound and feel very close to the wind and the trees.

"Thanks to eight days of plowing on the treasure itself, I discovered myself, the plow, the buffalo, the white clouds, and the plumeria trees behind the pagoda. Then one night in a dream, I saw father smiling at me. His face was radiant. 'It was Brother, not I, who discovered the treasure,' I told him.

"Since that day, I've lived freely, singing with the buffaloes, the cows, the fields, and the rice plants, awaiting your return. Now you are back, and I am very happy!"

The brother listened carefully to his sister's words, which came deeply from her heart. He understood that his sister had truly discovered the treasure. He had gotten close to the treasure once, but he had not reached it. Sometimes, he, too, felt that he did not long for the treasure anymore. He felt a close connection between the poem and himself, as close as his ancestors' blood circulating in his veins. He realized that he had not found the treasure because he was looking for it. His sister had found it because she had not intended to look for it. "Tomorrow morning," he thought, "I will walk down to the fields, see the old plow, the buffalo, and all of the treasures there, and I will find myself again."

Then he stood up and, filled with love and gratitude, he looked at his sister and walked with her up the hill. Together they drove the herd ahead of them. As they walked back to the farm, the brother felt the earth, the sky, and the wind as kind, loving arms embracing his whole being.

AFTERWORD

TWO FRIENDS, An and Dieu, were sitting in a little boat with an outboard motor chugging up the Thu Bon river in Central Vietnam. Four more little boats in the same party were chugging along one hundred yards behind. This was a contingent of small rescue boats organized by students to bring aid to flood victims. The five boats laden with sacks of rice, salt, and other necessities for relief work, were approaching the upper reaches of the Thu Bon River.

Looking at the vast stretch of river water, An said to Dieu, "This is a reenactment of the war between Son Vuong, Mountain King, and Thuy Vuong, Water King." The floodwaters had receded but not before more than eight hundred people had died. The number of buffalo, cattle, and other domestic animals that had lost their lives were too many to count.

As Dieu cast her eyes over the rice fields alongside the river, she said, "People generally take the side of Son Vuong and blame Thuy Vuong for the battle. In the struggle to gain the hand of the beautiful Mi Nuong, only the loser of the contest is condemned; the winner gets glory instead of blame."

An said, "Thuy Vuong was the one who caused the waters to rise so that he could fight Son Vuong. All Son Vuong did was protect himself."

"Somehow or other Son Vuong has to take some responsibility for the combat because he was one of the parties involved in it," Dieu replied.

"What do you want Son Vuong to do? Cut Mi Nuong in half and give half to Thuy Vuong?"

Dieu smiled. "It wouldn't be necessary to go as far as that. But brothers of one family have to find a way to reconcile. They can't come out and fight each other every year, destroying huge numbers of the population."

An looked up at Dieu and said, "I agree with you that the two of them have to find a way to reconcile. But what kind of reconciliation would it be? We can't force people to accept a decision that two brothers should live together with one wife, like Ong Tao, the Kitchen God."

Dieu laughed heartily. "Why not? As far as I see it, any way of resolving the conflict and putting an end to the slaughter of the people would be good."

"So you wouldn't feel sorry for Mi Nuong?" An queried.

"I would feel sorry for Mi Nuong. But now I'm feeling pity for the eight hundred of our compatriots who have just died because of this recent contest between Son Vuong and Thuy Vuong. I love Princess Sita who, because she loved her people, swallowed all the black poison that the sea monster had spewed out onto the surface of the ocean. I demand that the two kings find a way to reconcile, whatever that way might be. For the sake of the victims of the combat they cannot continue to fight."

"You plead your case very eloquently," said An. "I agree with you.

And both of us agree with Princess Sita. But what about the appearance of Princess Sita? Who knows if she will be admitted into the pantheon of Vietnamese gods."

"Why not?" Dieu responded. "Mythology is created by people. The people who lived long ago are like the people who live today. Myth was created to explain the universe and humanity's place in it. Myths are not simply creations of the imagination with no relation to reality. Princess Sita also reflects reality. In the present war, we have seen countless people working for reconciliation who face great danger and share the suffering of those who are wounded, just like Princess Sita. In the traditional telling of the battle between the gods Son Vuong and Thuy Vuong, the presence of someone like Sita has been forgotten. To remember her is to continue the work of creation. Without her, the story of Son Vuong and Thuy Vuong would not be complete."

"But if you do that, you could be criticized for embellishing an old story with new details," protested An.

"That doesn't really concern me, Brother An. Legends that have been handed down were not created by a single author. They came to be through a process of many generations adding something here and there, just like they did in the ballads and folksongs."

"In my opinion," An said, "creative additions should not be connections that falsify the truth and do not represent the peoples' aspirations. The names Sita and Nagaraja, for example, are not very Vietnamese."

"In ancient times, the territory of Vietnam was the meeting place of two civilizations: India and China," Dieu replied. "Therefore, characters like that of the goddess coming down from the world of Brahma, or the sacred garuda bird, Princess Sita of the sea palace, and makara, the sea monster of Indian legend, are acceptable. The influence of China on our culture has been so great that people forget about the influence of India and feel Chinese words are more Vietnamese than Sanskrit ones."

An smiled. "Acceptable or not, that is for the people to decide. We need to wait another two hundred years to see. We have to look both at legend and at history in order to discover historical truths.

"Do you know the story of the Hung king of Vietnam offering the white pheasant to the Chu king? In the time of the Chu dynasty in China, the Hung king of Vietnam ordered his ambassador to bring the white pheasant as a gift to the Chu king of China. The Chu king asked the ambassador why the people of Vietnam cut their hair short and tattooed their bodies, did not cover their heads and walked barefoot. After the ambassador had explained, the king asked why the ambassador had come. The ambassador answered: 'These past three years we have not had strong winds or continuous rain, and the four seas have been calm. We thought that a saint must have appeared in China, so we came to visit him.' The ambassador's words testify to his diplomatic skills and his deep understanding of the Chinese culture. A politician and man of culture like the Chu king would have naturally thought these words referred to himself. He had been planning to invade Vietnam, but after these words from the ambassador, he smiled and let the ambassador leave.

"What does this mean? Was it because of the ambassador's skillful words that the Chu king abandoned the idea of invading Vietnam? What is the point of the story? The gift of the white pheasant or the diplomacy that was part of the struggle for peace?"

Dieu sat still listening to An but she cast her eyes down at the water. She felt that she and An were on their way down to the Water Palace to ask the Dragon Prince to come up and resolve the problems of her country. She thought of Au Co's jar of miraculous medicine, about the mischievous Princess Sita, and suddenly she laughed.

"What are you laughing about?" asked An.

"I'm laughing at your eloquent sophistry. But never mind, our boat has arrived at Duc Duc.* Mr. Helmsman, which side do you want to come in on?"

The helmsman raised his voice in reply, "Either side is fine. We can find compatriots on either side."

An and Dieu stood up together, preparing to disembark.

---

*Duc Duc is a resettlement village just southwest of Danang in Central Vietnam. During the war it was in a heavily-contested combat zone and in 1971 the village was burned and its people massacred.

ABOUT THE CONTRIBUTORS

THICH NHAT HANH is a Vietnamese Buddhist monk. He was nominated by Dr. Martin Luther King, Jr. in 1967 for the Nobel Peace Prize. He is the author of the children's books *The Hermit and the Well*, *The Coconut Monk*, *A Pebble for Your Pocket*, and *Under the Rose Apple Tree*. He is also the author of books on mindfulness and engaged Buddhism, including *The Energy of Prayer, Calming the Fearful Mind*, and *Being Peace*. He lives in France, where he writes, teaches, and gardens. He also travels worldwide leading retreats on the art of mindful living.

MOBI WARREN was born in Minneapolis and raised in Texas. She is a meditation teacher, translator, and storyteller in San Antonio, where she lives with her two children, Emily and Bruce. Among the works of Thich Nhat Hanh she has translated into English are *The Miracle of Mindfulness, The Moon Bamboo, The Pine Gate, Old Path White Clouds: Walking in the Footsteps of the Buddha*, and *Hermitage among the Clouds*.

NGUYEN THI HOP AND NGUYEN DONG were both born in Vietnam. Since their marriage in 1968, they have collaborated on book and magazine covers, posters, and illustrations for over 100 titles published in Vietnam, Japan, Germany, France, and the United States. Their illustrations also appear in *Old Path White Clouds: Walking in the Footsteps of the Buddha* and *Hermitage among the Clouds*.

PARALLAX
PRESS

Parallax Press, a nonprofit publisher founded by Zen Master Thich Nhat Hanh, publishes books and media on the art of mindful living and Engaged Buddhism. We are committed to offering teachings that help transform suffering and injustice. Our aspiration is to contribute to collective insight and awakening, bringing about a more joyful, healthy, and compassionate society. For a copy of the catalog, please contact:

Parallax Press
P.O. Box 7355
Berkeley, CA 94707
parallax.org

Monastics and visitors practice the art of mindful living in the tradition of Thich Nhat Hanh at our mindfulness practice centers around the world. To reach any of these communities, or for information about how individuals, couples, and families can join in a retreat, please contact:

Plum Village
33580 Dieulivol, France
plumvillage.org

Deer Park Monastery
Escondido, CA 92026, USA
deerparkmonastery.org

Magnolia Grove Monastery
Batesville, MS 38606, USA
magnoliagrovemonastery.org

Blue Cliff Monastery
Pine Bush, NY 12566, USA
bluecliffmonastery.org

European Institute of
Applied Buddhism
D-51545 Waldbröl, Germany
eiab.eu

Thailand Plum Village
Nakhon Ratchasima
30130 Thailand
thaiplumvillage.org

The Mindfulness Bell, a journal of the art of mindful living in the tradition of Thich Nhat Hanh, is published three times a year by our community. To subscribe or to see the worldwide directory of Sanghas, or local mindfulness groups, visit **mindfulnessbell.org**.

The Thich Nhat Hanh Foundation supports Thich Nhat Hanh's peace work and mindfulness teachings around the world. For more information on how you can help or on how to nourish your mindfulness practice, visit the foundation at **tnhf.org**.